Matching Mr. Right

ALSO BY TAMRA BAUMANN

It Had to Be Him
It Had to Be Love
It Had to Be Fate
It Had to Be Them (Oct 2016)

Matching Mr. Right

TAMRA BAUMANN

This is a work of fiction. Names, characters, organizations, places, events, and incidents are either products of the author's imagination or are used fictitiously.

Text copyright © 2016 Tamra Baumann
All rights reserved.

ISBN 13: 978-0-9864479-4-5

No part of this book may be reproduced, or stored in a retrieval system, or transmitted in any form or by any means, electronic, mechanical, photocopying, recording, or otherwise, without express written permission of the publisher.

Published by Tamra Baumann

Cover design by: Clarissa Yeo

Printed in the United States of America

This book is dedicated to all my fellow Golden Heart© sisters and brothers. May all of your dreams come true.

1

> "Chester the monkey never meant to be bad . . . he just couldn't seem to help it."
> *Chester's Very Bad Day*

Shelby Marx narrowed her eyes, studying the man seated across from her. If he hired her to enhance his online dating image, she'd use words in his profile like *tall, rugged, outdoorsman* and *sports enthusiast*, because a body like his didn't come from a gym. His dark hair had subtle streaks of red from the sun, and his arresting blue eyes bored straight into one's soul.

Perfection—except for a slight bump on the bridge of his nicely proportioned nose. Probably broken in one of his manly pursuits. He'd be considered a ten on any woman's scale.

"So, why should I use your little online service when there are so many other options, Ms. Marx?"

Until he spoke.

Arrogance dropped Nick Caldwell's rating to a six. He'd been brusque and held a distinctly disinterested air from the moment they shook hands.

Ignoring his remark about her "little online service" she said, "I'm the best." She slid her brochure across the table and beamed a confident smile. "Why settle for less?"

He grunted in a caveman-like way before his dark-haired head lowered to study the brochure she'd designed for her matchmaking business, Cyrano at Your Service.

While waiting for his next rude response, Shelby drew in the rich aromas of coffee and buttery goodness as she studied the crowded café her best friend, Joann, had opened nine months earlier. Shelby's investment in Confections and Coffee gave her a forty percent ownership in the company. Maybe soon she'd start seeing some returns in actual dollars rather than in free coffee and turkey sandwiches. Then she could focus on writing children's books full time, and convincing the man she'd loved since she was fourteen to quit regarding her as nothing more than his little sister's best friend. Unrequited love stunk. But that would end soon, because she had a plan.

"Let me get this straight," the cave dweller spoke, drawing her attention back to their meeting. "I spend all night filling out a questionnaire that you'll use to tweak my online dating profiles, showing me in the best possible light. You filter the responses and arrange dates for the most promising women. And then, if I pay extra, you accompany me on the first meet? Like Cyrano? Standing in the bushes whispering words to help me woo a woman?" Laughing, he tossed the brochure aside.

His smile showed off perfect, straight, white teeth. He was a walking, and unfortunately talking, cliché. It just wasn't fair. Some of that perfection should've been spread around.

She sighed. "Standing in bushes isn't my idea of fun, so I usually opt to sit at a nearby table. By using tiny Bluetooth devices, I can listen to the conversation and then give my clients advice, helping them avoid those nasty lulls. But I don't think a guy like you would be interested in that part of my service."

His eyes narrowed. "What kind of guy do you think I am?"

Rude and stuck-up came to mind.

"Confident. I won't know what you're looking for in a woman until you spend *all night* filling out my form, but you don't strike me as someone who's seriously looking for his soul mate."

"Soul mate?" He snorted. "You're one of those?" He leaned closer and a wave of expensive, spicy aftershave filled the narrow space between them. "I'll bet you dream of the knight on a white charger who'll sweep you away to his castle so you can live happily ever after."

Yup, and her knight's name was Doctor Gregory Westin. He was due to return from a two-year stint with Doctors Without Borders next week. But the horse and castle she could live without. That'd just be overkill.

Shelby lifted her chin. "So, Mr. Caldwell, if you're not in search of true love, why *are* you here? My website and brochure say nothing about providing pimp or escort services."

He chuckled and leaned back in his chair. Studying her closely, he took a long sip from his coffee cup, as if contemplating the State of the Union rather than the answer to her simple question.

After sampling a bite of the chocolate chip cookie Shelby provided for all her first meetings, his eyes widened. "That's damned good!"

She half-expected him to say "ugh" or beat his chest in approval. Instead, Nick finished the cookie off in three normal-sized bites, then wiped his mouth on his napkin.

At least he had nice table manners.

"I don't need help in the sex department, Ms. Marx. I'm a realist. I'm not expecting to find love, just someone compatible who I can enjoy spending time with. I work a lot and have limited time to date." Then he shot her what seemed like his first genuine smile all day. "But if *you're* unattached . . . maybe we could just skip that long questionnaire?"

It took all her might to refrain from rolling her eyes. "I don't date clients."

"I haven't signed anything, so I'm not your client."

Nor would he be. She barely kept her head above water financially, but she had her standards. She didn't need the man's business that badly. Even if he was the most enticing piece of eye candy she'd ever met.

Shelby gathered her things and stood. When he stood as well, she held out her hand. "I'm sorry my little online service isn't what you're looking for. I wish you well, Mr. Caldwell. Goodbye."

He took her hand but didn't shake it. Instead, he gently held it as he gazed deeply into her eyes. Something in his expression changed from impudence to . . . respect? It sent an odd flutter to her stomach.

His mouth tilted into a slow grin. "No, I think you're just what I'm looking for, Shelby Marx. I'll fill out the questionnaire on your website tonight, and I'll even pay for the full package. It might be fun to hear your gravelly, sexy voice whispering in my ear." He gave her hand a soft squeeze, then turned to leave.

Shelby stared at his broad back draped in fine Italian silk as he shoved open the double glass doors and slapped on a pair of designer sunglasses. Why did a good-looking guy like him need her help?

What was he up to?

Nick started his Porsche and slipped out of his parking space. He could sense that Shelby had suspected his intentions weren't on the up-and-up, but he hadn't lied to her. He hadn't told a lie since his father walked out on their family, because of him, twenty years ago. Being in business, he'd learned to hold his cards to his chest, withhold certain facts, but to always tell the truth when asked a direct question. Doing otherwise could ruin people's lives. Like his mother's.

He'd filled out his real information on Shelby's interview sheet, so his charade wouldn't last forever, but spying on her might turn out to be the most fun he'd had in a long while.

Shelby's image tugged a smile from his lips as he merged into traffic. A sexy blonde pixie with a surprisingly deep, smoky voice, a pert nose, and the prettiest green eyes he'd ever seen. Even better, the woman had a backbone of steel. He admired that. She was half his size and yet didn't put up with any of the crap he'd thrown out to test her. She'd passed with flying colors.

Shelby Marx, of the obscenely wealthy Marx clan who'd amassed their fortune in Denver real estate, was one interesting woman. It didn't hurt that he'd enjoyed her company more than he'd had any other woman's in a very long time.

After asking one of Shelby's cousins about her and perusing the Net, he'd learned her aunt and uncle had raised her. No one seemed to know what happened to her parents. Or, no one was talking. Strange that a wealthy heiress like Shelby's mother could simply vanish off the face of the earth. Probably a lot more to that story, and it made Shelby an even greater mystery. One he'd enjoy solving.

He pulled into the underground parking lot at his office building and glided into his assigned spot. Now he just had to figure out what it was that made Shelby's business so successful. Shelby was his sister Lori's biggest competitor. He'd find out Shelby's business secrets the legal way, by becoming her client, and then make sure his sister's business became just as successful. Lori, recently widowed and too stubborn to ask for help, ran her online matchmaking service with her heart—the business part wasn't her priority, but it needed to be.

He'd promised his grandmother the night she died that he'd help Lori's business thrive, thereby keeping the long line of matchmakers on their mother's side of the family alive. Grams said Lori's daughter, his niece, Emily, had the "gift" too, so it was his job to be sure there was a business to pass down. How Grams could tell that a six-year-old had the "gift" seemed a little nuts, but a promise was a promise, so he'd keep it. And what his sister didn't know wouldn't hurt her, so he'd had to resort to fixing her business behind her back.

Fixing things is what he did best.

As he exited his car and headed for the tenth floor, a familiar Disney ringtone sounded from his suit coat. He reached for his cell and answered with "Hello, your highness."

Emily, who had recently declared she'd planned to be a princess when she grew up, giggled. "Hi, Uncle Nick. Mommy said to remind you how hard it is for single mommies to be in two places at the same time before I ask you something."

"Put your mother, the blackmailer, on the phone, Em."

After a moment, and a brief discussion with Emily, Lori said, "Thanks a lot. First you buy a six-year-old a cell phone just because she asked, and now I have to explain to her what blackmail is?"

"Serves you right." Nick walked through the glass doors, waved to the receptionist, then headed toward his office. "But all you have to do is tell her it's what you do to me anytime you want a favor." He pulled off his suit coat and tossed it on the leather couch in his office before loosening his tie. "Make it quick. I'm busy."

"Yeah, yeah, busy killing people's hopes and dreams when you tell them they aren't necessary to the company's bottom line. Doing something noble for a change will be good for your blackened soul."

"How about all those jobs people get to *keep* when I save said business from failing?" He wiggled his mouse and called up his e-mail. It was his job to restructure businesses. Sometimes that meant jobs had to be cut. "My soul's as white as the driven snow."

"White as the . . ." His sister's snort of disbelief mixed with the sounds of tapping on a keyboard. "So, anyway, I have a meeting and you're my last resort. Emily's looked forward to the Chester book signing all week. If you refuse, you'll be responsible for her little broken heart. Not that you're unaccustomed to breaking women's hearts."

"Hey, I haven't broken anyone's heart in years. I actually had a steady relationship for the past two years, remember?" Beth had broken things off a month ago because she'd been working nonstop on a big case and her career came first. He totally got that. No hard feelings.

"That wasn't a real relationship by anyone's standards. And she's playing the oldest trick in the book by breaking up with you and hoping you'll miss her. She's in love with you and waiting for you to grow up and realize you're not like Dad."

He'd never be like his cheating father. Causing the kind of pain he watched his mother go through. He saw no benefits to marriage and kids. Especially after the hurt his father had caused his family.

And Beth, in love with him? Nope. They'd had rules. They'd been free to date others, but if they slept with someone else, the deal between them was over. Beth was a busy lawyer and she'd wanted the same thing he did. Uncomplicated, monogamous sex without the messy emotions. It had served them both well for their time together. Lori was just trying to guilt him into taking Em.

"Beth knew I'll never marry, so your theory is full of cra—"

"Says you. So, I'll drop Em off at your office tomorrow at about three thirty, then all you have to do is take her to the bookstore by the mall. It starts at four."

He'd had to do worse things growing up in a house full of women. If he could buy emergency tampons and pink nail polish, he could probably handle a trip to the bookstore with his niece.

After a quick look at his schedule he added some bite to his bark. "I'll expect to be fed after!"

"Deal. But don't expect anything fancy."

"Fine." Before his sister could think of any other errands for him to run, he disconnected the call. Lori hated when he hung up on her. He could visualize the scowl on her face as she slapped the phone down. No one was more fun to tease. She'd surely find a way to retaliate.

He looked forward to it.

Chuckling, he got to work blackening his soul by saving businesses from certain death.

❦

Shelby sat on her living room couch, her feet propped on the coffee table, tapping away at the keys on her laptop. She'd been off-kilter ever since her meeting with Nick Caldwell that morning, so it didn't surprise her that she'd just written Chester, the mischievous little monkey in her books, firmly into a corner. One he couldn't get out of even if he stacked a ton of bananas on top of each other.

She turned toward Joann, who sat at the opposite end of the couch. Shelby needed a jolt of inspiration or maybe a random idea that Jo always seemed able to provide. Her best friend, roommate, and now business partner, suddenly broke out in hysterical laughter at the *Real Housewives of Somewhere* on TV. Shelby hated those shows because the women who starred in them all reminded her of her cold, narcissistic aunt Victoria.

Rather than distract Jo from her fun, Shelby decided to call it a night. The solution would come to her by morning—hopefully. Her editor had her on tight deadlines, demanding three new books next year, and each one had to do better than the last. It was the only way it'd get her series off the mid-list and onto the bestseller list.

But making it onto a list wasn't why she wrote books about an impish monkey who was always in trouble. She wanted to send the message that mistakes and accidents happen, and that kids need to learn to forgive themselves for them.

Fortunately, most kids didn't have as much forgiving to do as she did. The scars left after Shelby had accidentally killed her parents and sister with her carelessness ran deeper than those the accident left on her legs. But if she could save just one kid from the guilt she felt everyday, it'd be worth all her efforts, no matter if she made the bestseller list or not.

As she was about to shut down for the night, her computer dinged, announcing an incoming e-mail from her Cyrano site. Eager to push away her unwanted thoughts of scars and guilt, she opened the message.

It was from *him*.

Clicking on the attachment, she scanned the pages before her. Nick had been true to his word, he'd paid for the full package. His face, in all its annoying perfection, beamed at her from the photos he attached. His questionnaire was completely filled out, and he provided all of his passwords to the social network and dating sites she'd suggested he join so she could edit them. Now the ball was in her court.

She'd googled Nick before she'd met with him and had found he was a year older than her at thirty, and he owned a successful business consulting firm. Nick seemed to be telling the truth about himself and his finances. She'd seen the Porsche he'd driven off in earlier, a similar model to the one she used to own before she'd sold it, deciding to live off of her own earnings, not the money controlled by her aunt and uncle.

Scanning Nick's preferences in women, Shelby laughed. "Remember the annoying guy from this morning, Jo?"

"Who could forget?" Jo appeared by Shelby's side instantly. "Is this the handsome caveman's questionnaire?"

"Yeah. You're gonna love it."

Grinning, Jo grabbed the computer and placed it on her lap. "He likes his women tall, so that lets you out."

"I'm crushed." Shelby placed a hand over her heart. "But that's good for you, Amazon girl."

"Yes, it is." Jo's eyes lit with excitement until she saw the next two items. "Seriously? He wants a blonde with big boobs? The guy has no imagination whatsoever. He should expand to brunettes with normal-sized breasts. They're the best in bed. I read a magazine quiz confirming that, by the way."

Shelby nodded and worked to keep a solemn look on her face. "Undoubtedly. But don't stop reading now."

Jo's eyes lit with outrage. "The man *cannot* be serious!"

Nick wanted the impossible. A blonde bombshell who liked to camp, play sports, watch sports, go to brew pubs, and he'd like her to bake for him. He loved sweets.

Shelby chuckled. "Only Nick's dream girl could slam the game-winning pitch out of the park while not breaking a sweat. Then the team would celebrate at the nearest sports bar, where she'd push the cook out of the way and prepare the best pub grub known to mankind for Nick and his buddies. After that, they'd sit around reminiscing about the game she helped win and drink all those heavy, dark beers, not giving a second thought to maintaining that perfect figure of hers. Then she'd whisper in Nick's ear how much she looked forward to their planned camping trip because she just adored skinny-dipping under waterfalls."

Jo leaned closer to the screen. "He has skinny-dipping on his list?"

"No." Shelby laughed. "But I think we've just about covered every fifteen-year-old's idea of the perfect woman."

"Good luck with this one." Jo shook her head and handed the computer back. "Actually, if it weren't for the tall part, and the big chest, Nick might just fall for *you*." Jo batted her eyes, mimicking a proper Southern belle. "Shelby Marx, you're just about the cutest tomboy God ever placed on this earth."

Shelby rolled her eyes. "I just hope your brother can forget that part and see me as a woman after all these years, not the girl they used to let play football with the boys after school."

Jo smiled sweetly and patted Shelby's arm. "You were the fastest little wide receiver in the neighborhood, Shelby, and the only girl who ever wanted to play with those rough boys. That might be a little hard for Greg to forget. But I'll put in a good word for you. I'd love to see you guys end up together because then we'd be real sisters, not just of the heart." Jo gave her a shoulder bump. "'Nite, Tomboy."

"'Nite, Stick." Letting out a long sigh, Shelby mumbled, "Please let Greg be the first to truly overlook the scars on my legs."

2

"Always telling the truth is really hard to do, especially for Chester the monkey."
Liar, Liar, Chester's Pants are on Fire

Shelby glanced up from her laptop and scowled at Nick as he sauntered toward her across the busy café. The man was over an hour late and hadn't even had the decency to call.

He folded his long body onto the chair next to hers. Then he blessed her with one of his don't-you-think-I'm-adorable smiles. "My meeting ran long and I'm starving. What's good today?"

Really? Not an "I'm sorry" or a "Hi how are you?"

"Manners are selling well today. You should get a double helping. You could use them."

He chuckled. "Sorry I kept you waiting—"

Shelby raised a finger and pointed to her Bluetooth earpiece before activating her mic. She was helping a client two tables away and the conversation had slowed.

"Ask what she loves most about her best friend." That got Randy's date, a cute redhead, smiling and gushing, so Shelby sipped her skinny latte and called up Nick's Facebook page on her computer.

"I have something later this afternoon, so I'm going to try to help you and Randy at the same time. Let's start with these bromance pictures of you and your buddies flinging yourselves off things attached to bungee cords and ropes. Oh, and let's not forget the mandatory group photos afterward celebrating your braveness with red plastic cups filled with beer."

Nick leaned closer and threw his arm around the back of her chair.

Man, he smelled good.

"But that's what I do." He brushed his mouth against her ear and sent a quiver up her spine. "I've gotten lots of e-mails—with naked pictures attached—from these photos. Women like sweaty guys in tight shirts with all our muscles showing."

She leaned away, disgusted with herself for momentarily wanting to feel those big muscles too. "Unless you've got aspirations to be a Chippendale dancer—"

"Dancing's not my thing."

"Or a gigolo, we're getting rid of some of these skin shots, pal."

"The gigolo I could do." Nick grinned. "But you already told me you won't be my pimp, so I'd have to find someone else if I went that route."

After Shelby sent him a long sideways look, he said, "Okay. Whatever you say, Dating Master."

She deleted most of the pictures and then added some of the professional headshots he'd provided. "Do you have any group family shots? That'd send a nice vibe." And it'd be interesting to see if the rest of his family was as pretty as him.

"I'm sure I could find some." Nick checked his Rolex. "Really, what's good to eat?"

Shelby shushed him again so she could talk to Randy. "Ask her—"

"If she prefers baths or showers," Nick blurted out.

"No, don't!" Shelby jumped up and moved to the other side of the table. "Ask what her all-time favorite movie is."

Sitting safely across from Nick, Shelby sent Randy an apologetic smile. Satisfied the conversation was back on track, she said to Nick, "I'm guessing you're a meat eater. The pulled pork's amazing."

"Pulled pork it is." Nick stood and weaved his big body through the tables. His suit, cut a little tighter than yesterday's, showed off his big shoulders—and his rear end? Nice. He'd be a pretty decent gigolo at that.

When Nick slapped Randy on the back, Shelby's heart nearly stopped. Nick beamed a bright smile at her confused client. "Nice to see you, man."

What was he up to? Would he blow Randy's cover?

Shelby whispered, "Just go with it, Randy. His name's Nick." Then she hopped up to move Nick along before he could do any more damage.

She stopped in her tracks when Nick introduced himself to Randy's date and then proceeded to sing Randy's praises.

Shelby let out the breath she'd been holding in as Nick told Randy to call him, then excused himself and made his way toward the order counter.

Sitting down again, she listened as Randy's date said, "I have to get back to work, but this was fun. I'd really like to see you again—if you would?"

The shy smile that lit Randy's handsome face made Shelby's day. And when he took the opportunity to nail down a time before she could prompt him to do so, it made her proud. He was finally getting the hang of it. Another check in the win box. Yes!

Randy sent her a thumbs up behind his back as he walked his date out to her car.

Leaning back in her chair, she yanked the Bluetooth from her ear as she contemplated Nick's actions. Had he done that to be nice, or obnoxious? It might have been just the nudge Randy's date needed. To think Randy was friends with a smooth talking, handsome guy like Nick.

What the heck was Nick up to? He didn't need her. He could have any woman he wanted.

A southwestern grilled-chicken salad suddenly appeared before her along with a frosty glass of her favorite strawberry iced tea.

Nick sat across from her and unloaded his lunch tray. He not only got the pulled pork sandwich and a pile of fat steak-cut fries, but chocolate-mousse pie and an éclair. How could he eat like that and still have all those bulging muscles instead of a pot-belly?

Stop thinking about those pictures!

"Thanks." Digging her wallet from her purse she pulled out a ten wondering how he'd just happened to pick her favorite salad. "Lucky guess or are you a creepy stalker?"

He waved her money away. "Since you appear to office here, I asked the lady at the counter if she knew what you liked best. She told me she'd take care of it. After paying your full fee last night, I might have taken your money, but I was afraid she'd tell you and then you'd think I was a jerk."

Too late—she knew he was a jerk. But a paying-client jerk, so she kept her yap shut.

"Smart move. Jo and I have each other's backs."

He nodded as he swiped a fat fry through a puddle of ketchup. "She mentioned you two go way back?"

"Yup. We were neighbors growing up and then went to the same college."

"Have you found her a soul mate yet?"

"Maybe it's me." Shelby batted her eyes at him.

Nick sputtered into his Coke but quickly recovered. "Nope. You're definitely into men." He took another drink then laid his glass down, studying her intently. "So, have you found Jo the man of her dreams?"

She took a bite of her salad, making him wait for her response. "She's not in the market at the moment. She's concentrating on this café."

Why were they sharing small talk? The man deserved payback for nearly giving her a heart attack. She shouldn't do it, but like her favorite mischievous monkey, Chester, she couldn't help herself. "But Jo often peruses magazine articles about relationships and dating. Just last night, she mentioned she'd read a survey of men who claimed brunettes were better in bed than blondes." She smiled sweetly as she took a slug of iced tea. "Any thoughts on that, Mr. Caldwell?"

His brows furrowed as he contemplated his answer. "Those quizzes are bogus, but because you're a blonde and my momma drowned all the dumb kids in our family, no comment."

She laughed despite herself. "How many of those kids survived?"

"I have two older sisters. You?"

"I had a younger sister, but she died a long time ago." A familiar arrow of pain stabbed at Shelby's heart. She still missed Sarah like it was yesterday, not the twenty-two-years ago she'd lost her baby sister. And her parents too.

Nick's sandwich stopped halfway to his lips. "Sorry. My sisters can be a real pain in the ass sometimes . . . but mostly they make me glad they're mine."

Glad they're mine? Maybe Nick wasn't a complete Neanderthal.

They ate in silence for a few minutes until Shelby just couldn't stand not knowing any longer. "Why did you stop by Randy's table?"

He shrugged. "Women have all the power in a first meet. They get to decide if you get a second chance. Never hurts to have a wingman."

"Hummm" was all she could manage. So he was being nice to Randy? A puzzle—no, a contradiction. That's what Nick Caldwell was.

He finished off his pie and then started on the éclair. After he had devoured every last crumb, he stood and threw a five on the table for a tip. "Ignore my questionnaire and set me up with a brunette. Probably should test out Jo's theory." He shot her a naughty grin then headed for the door.

࿇

Nick glanced at his niece as they drove to the bookstore. He was no expert, but something was wrong. Her face was scrunched up and she kept rubbing her stomach. "You okay there, Princess? 'Cuz if there's going to be ralphing involved I'd rather you didn't do it in my Porsche."

Emily forced a smile. "I'm just excited."

"I'd be excited too, to meet my favorite author in the entire universe. That Chester dude's fun. I like him."

Emily's face brightened. "Me too!"

"You sure you're feeling okay?" He pulled into a parking space.

"Yup." Emily whipped off her seatbelt and opened the door.

Nick helped her out and then held her hand as they crossed the parking lot. Emily's pace was especially pokey, so he scooped her up into his arms. "Come on, lead feet. Let's get us a Chester book."

When Emily tucked her head under his chin and closed her eyes, it confirmed it. The kid was sick. He turned back toward the car. "Maybe we'd better get that book some other time. When you're feeling better."

Emily's little head popped up and she wailed, "Noooo! I *have* to get the new Chester book! Pleeeease Uncle Nick?"

"Okay, pipe down. So here's what we'll do. Pick up the book, get it signed, then get right back out. No messing around. Deal?" He held out his fist for a knuckle bump.

Emily's face lit up a fraction as she fist-bumped him. "Deal."

After he left his sister a voice mail telling her Em was sick and asking if he should take her to the doctor, Nick opened the door to the tiny bookstore.

It was crowded and smelled of leather and dust.

He withheld a curse at the long line ahead of them. Em was miserable. They needed to get the book as quick as possible. Craning his neck, he counted fifteen adults with at least one kid in tow waiting for an autograph.

He needed a plan.

When he spotted a harried looking mother with three kids, he considered playing on her maternal sympathies to get Emily a better place in line. But then he found their fast-track ticket.

She was tall, blonde, dressed in designer clothes, talking on the phone, and ignoring her kid. Even better, her left hand, the one that held the phone, didn't sport a wedding ring.

Nick slid past the others in line and moved beside her. "Hi."

She glanced up, smiled, then hung up without saying goodbye. "Hello." She glanced at his left hand splayed on Emily's back, the one he'd purposely left there to display his own lack of wedding ring. "I'm Judith. And you are?"

"Nick. And this is my niece, Emily." He accepted Judith's outstretched hand and shook it. Her hand was much larger and cooler than Shelby's dainty one he'd held the day before. "I've got a problem. Em here's not feeling so good. I don't know if she'll be able to wait out this long line."

Right on cue, Emily whimpered, "I *can't* go until I get the new Chester book." Em was good. He had to give it to her. They made a great team.

Judith glanced down at the kid beside her. "I'm sure Samantha wouldn't mind letting you cut in front of us. Especially if Emily isn't feeling well."

The little girl, a miniature version of her mother in designer clothes, frowned. "Yes, I would. We've been waiting—"

Judith nudged the kid with her elbow. "It'll be fine. So, Nick." She eyed his suit. "What kind of job allows you time to play hooky with your niece?"

He figured he'd only have to keep up the small talk for about ten more minutes, and then they could get the heck out. Emily fell sound asleep and drooled on his shoulder as he talked with Miss Designer Shoes. When he glanced ahead to check their progress, his gaze landed on Shelby.

She was the author of the Chester books?

By day she helped people find love, and by night she wrote kids' books? Something about that seemed a little . . . strange. But intriguing.

He hadn't been able to stop thinking about her since he left her a few hours before. Too bad she was the white-picket-fence, kids-and-a-dog type, or he'd be tempted to tear up his contract and ask her out for real. But then his grandmother's dying words, begging him to save Lori's business, shut down that thought.

Shelby glanced up and saw him, then her forehead crumpled in confusion. He lifted his hand in greeting.

She sent him a deep frown before turning her attention back to the kid who stood in front of her. When Shelby smiled at the kid, her whole face lit up. She'd never smiled at him like that. Probably because he'd been acting like a jerk as he spied on her. He wanted to be her most challenging client, hopefully revealing all the tricks Shelby had in her toolbox.

But, man, he was a sucker for a cute blonde with a great smile.

Shelby forced her attention back to the sweet kid who stood before her. What was Nick doing and where did he get the kid who was asleep on his shoulder? His profile didn't list any children, and the way the lady beside him smiled and flirted with him, it was obvious he needed no help whatsoever from her "little online service." Maybe he really was a stalker. She'd have to ask Jo if she and Nick actually had that conversation about the salad at the café like he'd said.

She signed a book and slid it back to the little girl named Lauren. "Thanks for coming to meet me today. I hope you like the story."

Lauren's blue eyes twinkled with joy. "I love everything Chester does. He's the best. Thank you."

"You're welcome." Gotta love a kid with manners. After waving to Lauren's mother, a new family moved in front of her.

Nick was next after them. She could feel the warm sweep of his eyes on her as she signed two books for the cute twins standing before her named Lilly and Lindsey. Nick had a way of studying her, as if he could see deeply inside, searching for her heavily guarded secrets.

It bugged.

When it was Nick's turn, she didn't bother to greet him. Instead she cocked a brow and waited for his explanation. She ignored the flip her stomach made as he stood in front of her looking like sin on a stick. Her inner bad girl begged for just one lick.

But Nick was a shallow, no-strings-attached kind of guy. The opposite of Greg. The man she'd waited two years for.

Nick beamed one of his big smiles. "Hello, Summer Sinclair. Seems you're a woman of many hidden talents?"

"You too." She slid her gaze to the child asleep on Nick's shoulder. "Seems you forgot to add single parent to your profile."

"This is my niece." He nudged the sleeping girl on his shoulder. "Emily, wake up. Let's get Shelby to sign your book."

The darling, curly-dark-haired girl yawned and blinked like a baby owl. "Who's Shelby?" The girl's cheeks were unnaturally red, as if flushed with fever.

Alarmed, Shelby stood and reached across the table to lay the back of her hand on the child's forehead. It burned under her touch. Nick had a very sick kid on his hands. Something like that had to cramp his style as he flirted with the obviously smitten woman behind him in line.

Shelby tucked a clump of stray curls that had fallen across the little girl's forehead behind her ear, exposing the same startling blue eyes as her irritating uncle's. "Poor baby. You're not feeling so good, huh?"

Nick said, "Emily's a huge fan and couldn't be persuaded to stay home in bed where she belongs. Nice pen name by the way." He leaned closer and whispered, "Kinda sexy."

That did it.

She huffed out a breath and signed Emily's book. She wanted Nick out of her face as quickly as possible. He was the epitome of the kind of man she usually avoided: all handsome, arrogant, and self-confident. Something her hormones were having trouble remembering they didn't like. It'd probably be best if they didn't work together.

As she handed the book to Emily, she said, "It must be tough to have such a smarty-pants uncle, Emily. I hope you feel better soon."

Emily worked up a small giggle. "That's what momma says about him too."

"Traitor!" Nick's warm smile proved he clearly loved the child. "Keep it up and I'm taking the cell phone back." He slid another book from the pile. "I'd like one too, *Summer*."

Before Shelby could refuse, a gorgeous, dark-haired, feminine version of Nick rushed to his side. "Sorry, I just got your message. I came as fast as I could." She took Emily from his shoulder. "Come here, honey." Then she turned and stuck her hand out to Shelby. "Hi, I'm Emily's mom, Lori. We just adore your books. It's a pleasure to meet you."

"Thank you. So, Nick is your . . . brother?"

Lori nodded. "Yes. Are you two friends?"

Shelby said, "No," at the same time Nick said, "Yes."

Lori frowned at her brother. "What have you done now, Nick?"

Nick met Shelby's gaze and winced. Suddenly he looked like a kid caught climbing through his bedroom window after curfew instead of his normal arrogant self.

"Nothing. Let's go. See you, Shelby." Nick wrapped his arm around his sister's waist and tugged.

The sexy blonde woman behind them called out, "Nick, wait. Here's my number."

Nick stopped his hasty retreat. "Great, thanks." He accepted the piece of paper and then sent Shelby a pained look. "Um . . . so I'll call you?"

Her jaw clenched. If she weren't in a store packed full of kids who looked up to her, she'd tell Nick to take a hike. "I'll call you. *Please* don't call *me*."

3

> "Asking for help when you're in trouble is hard to do . . . especially for bad little monkeys."
> *Chester's Disastrous Day at The Zoo*

Tired of sitting on the couch tapping away at her keyboard, Shelby yawned and stretched her hands over her head. She needed a break from Chester and his antics. Was it her imagination, or was Chester acting particularly naughty in this book? She might have to clean up his act a bit. Chester was starting to operate like Nick.

Worse, she hadn't slept well the night before. Visions of Nick and his muscles from the Facebook pictures had bounced around her brain all night. Nick and Greg were the only men her body had reacted to in such a visceral way. Now she was even dreaming about the Neanderthal's smile.

She'd call Nick later, tell him she wasn't the right matchmaker for him, then give him a full refund. She wouldn't want an unhappy customer as successful as Nick out there talking poorly about her, so maybe she'd offer to set him up on one meet for free before they went their separate ways.

The only good thing about her inability to sleep because of Nick, was that it helped her figure out how to fix her story.

A loud knock sounded on her front door.

She laid her computer on the coffee table and crossed to the entry. Standing on her tiptoes, she peered through the peephole.

No freaking way. It was *him*. And he looked like crap.

She didn't think that was possible.

He wore the same suit as the day before, now rumpled, his jaw covered with day-old stubble. His hair was a mess, as if he'd been running his hands through it.

She picked up the bat she kept in the entry and yanked the door open. Thankfully a locked glass storm door still separated them. "Go away, or I'm calling the police."

"Good. You're home. I have an emergency." He blinked at her as his smile grew. "You wear glasses? Cute."

She forgot she had them on. And she was wearing dumpy sweats.

Nice.

Clutching her bat tighter, she said, "How did you get my address?"

"I know your cousin, Jake. We belong to the same climbing club. Small world, huh? Anyway, he gave it to me. And since you told me not to call . . ."

She breathed out a sigh and lowered the bat. If Jake trusted Nick enough to give him her address, then Nick wasn't a horrible person. Just an annoying one. She unlocked the door so they wouldn't have to yell through the glass and pushed it open. "So, you're having a dating emergency?"

"No, it's my niece, Emily. She's in the hospital."

Shelby's anger instantly dissipated. "What's wrong?"

"Appendix. They got her into surgery just in time last night. Em's uncomfortable this morning, but mostly she's scared of dying, leaving her mom all alone. Her father was killed while in the military, fighting overseas. Emily's got issues."

Issues? Only someone who hadn't lost a parent, especially at such a young age, could call what Emily was feeling *issues*. It's heartbreak. "I'd be happy to help Emily. *You're* lucky I asked questions first before I beat you with my bat. I thought you were a stalker."

"I'm not a stalker, Shelby." He sent her one of his sexy grins. "But if you'll help Emily, I'll let you take a free swing. She's inconsolable because she can't find the book you signed for her. She had it with her when they admitted her, but it's disappeared in the shuffle last night. Will you sign another for her? Please?"

The man said *please*? Would wonders never cease?

She held the door open wider. "Fine. Come in. And if you'll wait while I change, I'll deliver it in person. I have a little experience at being a kid in the hospital."

Relief softened his face. "Thank you, Shelby. I owe you one."

"And I won't let you forget it." She let go and the spring loaded door slapped closed behind him.

Nick looked ready to drop at any moment. She shouldn't offer him anything because she really didn't want to encourage him, but she had manners. Maybe he'd learn by example. "Have a seat. Want some coffee?"

He sighed and dropped onto the couch. "More than I want to draw my next breath."

She beamed her sweetest, fake smile. "Too bad I'm out of arsenic, or I might have been tempted to arrange that."

She left him on the couch and went to the kitchen to get his coffee. As she poured him a cup, she remembered he'd liked her chocolate chip cookies from their first meeting, so she grabbed two from the cookie jar and put them on a plate. When she returned to the living room, Nick was smiling and tapping the down arrow key on her laptop.

Rude!

"What are you doing?"

"Sorry. I couldn't resist. Your Chester books rock. This is the best one yet." He gulped his coffee, then ate a cookie as he read. The sincere smile on his face made him even sexier, dammit . . . and that he liked her books didn't hurt.

But then, of course he liked them. Chester was acting as badly as Nick.

She shook her head and then went to get ready.

After a few minutes, he called out, "Can I have some more coffee?"

"Last I checked, you had two hands," she yelled back from her bedroom. "Get it yourself!"

Maybe she shouldn't have said that about his hands. He'd think she was checking out the size of them to gauge the size of his other . . . parts. She'd be more careful about that.

After she put her contacts in, touched up her makeup, and combed her hair, she changed out of her favorite writing sweats into jeans and a sweater. It had been an unusually warm fall, so she'd forgo a coat.

After grabbing one of her latest books from the box her publisher had sent, she signed it, then added an extra get well wish. Ready to roll, she went to find Nick.

He sat on the couch with his arms crossed, his chin resting on his chest, sound asleep. She glanced at the screen of her laptop, relieved he'd fallen asleep at the end of her story instead of the middle.

She couldn't fight the urge that overcame her. Really, her middle name should be Chester. She leaned down and shouted in his ear, "All ready to go!"

Nick jerked upright and banged his knee on the coffee table.

"Dammit, Shelby!" He ran a hand through his hair and glowered at her.

"What?" She plastered on an innocent smile. "How was I to know you're such a light sleeper?"

❦

When they got to the hospital, Nick held the door open for Shelby. Guilt clawed inside his gut for spying on her. Especially when she hadn't hesitated to help Emily. He'd been tempted to dig through Shelby's computer when he'd had the chance, but he couldn't be that underhanded. He'd just stuck to asking probing questions about her business during their drive to the hospital.

Now to keep Shelby and Lori apart so she wouldn't accidentally blow his cover. It had been a close call at the book signing. Luckily Lori used her married last name for her business, not Caldwell, so Shelby wouldn't recognize Lori as her competitor. And hopefully his sister wasn't back yet after going home to get Em's favorite doll.

They turned toward the elevators, but after a few steps Shelby wasn't beside him like she'd been a moment before. Her pale face made him rush to her side and grab her arm. He led her to a nearby bank of chairs. "What's wrong?"

"Nothing." She lowered her head between her knees.

"Deep breaths, Shelby." She probably wouldn't appreciate comfort from him. But he hated feeling so helpless.

Taking the risk, he slowly ran his hand up and down her back, testing the waters. She tensed at first, but relaxed a little as he continued his soft strokes, waiting her out.

While growing up, he'd had more than his share of calming upset women. As an adult, he'd made it a point to avoid upset women at all costs. But he owed Shelby, so he sucked it up.

When his fingers gently massaged the tense muscles in her long, kissable neck, she sighed.

Progress.

Her breathing became more steady, so he said, "I think we may have gotten off to a bad start, but—"

Shelby snorted as her color returned a bit. "Ya think?"

"My sisters tell me I'm a pretty good listener."

She sent him a smoldering look, but as he stared deeply into her pretty green eyes, he couldn't help the smile that tilted his lips. She was beautiful, even though she wanted to beat the crap out of him with her bat.

"Stop that! I'm not like other women. You can't charm me with that you-know-you-want-me smile of yours." Shelby frowned and looked away.

Just when he thought he'd been shut down, she whispered, "When I was a kid, I lost my family and then spent almost a year in and out of the hospital. Being here, the smell, it sometimes conjures all the bad memories from back then."

He took her hand and gently squeezed. "What happened?"

She glanced at their entwined fingers and blew out a long resigned breath. "When I was seven, I'd missed dinner one night, so I sneaked to the kitchen and made myself a grilled cheese sandwich. After I ate it, I went back to bed. I awoke later to a house filled with smoke. I must've forgotten to turn off the stove, although I swear I remember turning the knob off. Then I heard my little sister crying, so I ran down the hall to her room and pulled her out of her crib. I tried to open her window, but it was stuck and I couldn't lift it. I finally got it open a little so I held my sister out so she could breathe, but the window crashed down on my back and I got trapped. I woke up later in the hospital and found out my legs had been burned from about here"—Shelby pointed to a place mid-thigh—"to my feet. I had over twenty surgeries to repair my skin."

So that's how she'd lost her family. It was obvious she still blamed herself for it, just as he blamed himself for the destruction of his parents' marriage. Although, in contrast, his pain couldn't match hers. "I'm sorry, Shelby. I'll take you home."

She shook her head and stood. "I'm good now. Let's go."

"Okay. But just say the word and we're gone." He wrapped his arm around her shoulder and pulled her close. She still looked kind of wobbly.

"Thanks. But you still owe me!"

He chuckled. "I had no doubt."

When they got to Emily's room, Nick's mom, who was seated by Emily's bed, sent them a strained smile. Things must've not improved much since he'd left. Em's lunch tray hadn't been touched and the little worry line in the middle of her forehead was deeper than he'd ever seen it. She had a death grip on the doll Lori ran home to get, so where was his sister? "Hi, Mom. This is Shelby."

His mom stood and shook Shelby's hand. "Nice to meet you. We're all fans of yours. Lori will be sorry she missed you."

"Thank you, Mrs. Caldwell. It's nice to meet you too." Shelby smiled that cute smile at his mom that he'd only seen when Shelby looked at kids. Apparently everyone but him got that smile.

His mom turned to him. "Lori just stepped out to get us some lunch. She'll be back in a bit."

Thank God for that. Maybe they could be in and out before Lori got back.

Shelby sat beside Emily on her bed. "How are you doing kiddo?"

Emily worked up a sad smile that poked at his heart. "I lost your book."

"No problem. I brought you another." Shelby pulled out a book from her ginormous purse.

"Thank you, Summer." Emily's eyes lit with joy.

"You're welcome." Shelby tossed her purse onto a nearby chair. "But you can call me Shelby. Summer Sinclair is a pen name. Sometimes people who write books have to use a different name than their own because theirs doesn't sound as good, or someone else already writes under that name. Or, sometimes, you belong to a family who doesn't like that you write kids' books, so you have to change it for them."

Emily's brows knit. "But if you have two names, how do you remember when you should be Summer and when you should be Shelby?"

"That's the tricky part." Shelby reached out and wrapped one of Emily's hands in hers. "I hear you've been feeling a little scared about being in the hospital. How come?"

Nick leaned against the wall and crossed his arms. Why wouldn't Shelby's family be proud of what she did? Shelby's books were fantastic. His favorite to read to Em whenever he tucked her in.

Emily glanced at Nick's mother. "People die in the hospital. I don't want my mommy to be all alone if I died like my daddy did."

Shelby gave Em a quick hug. "You've already done the hard part. You've had your surgery and now you're fine. Most of the time, people get *better* in hospitals. I missed a whole school year when I was just a little older than you because I had to have a lot of surgeries to make the skin on my legs better after an accident."

"Do they still hurt?" Emily reached out and rubbed Shelby's leg.

"No." Shelby covered Emily's hand with hers once more. "Actually, they're sort of numb. But I'm all better now, just like you'll be tomorrow or the day after."

His mother leaned down and kissed Emily's forehead. "See? Shelby says everything's going to be fine too, and it will. Now, why don't you try to eat some lunch?"

Shelby poked around Emily's untouched lunch tray that held a sandwich and some applesauce. "They usually have a secret stash of desserts for the kids who eat their lunch, you know. The nurses just don't tell you about that unless you ask."

"Really?" Emily perked right up at that.

"Yup. All you have to do is press the button and they come. But you have to ask really nice." Shelby found the call switch and handed it to Emily. "Chester would love to have all the ice cream and pudding he could eat, don't you think?"

Emily pressed the button. "Maybe you should write a Chester book about being in the hospital, Shelby."

"That's a great idea. Maybe you could help me. What kind of things do you think Chester would do to get into trouble?"

Emily pursed her lips, as if in deep thought. "He'd probably turn the TV up real loud, jump on the bed, and then see what kind of things he could stuff down the toilet. And he'd definitely sneak ice cream and pudding from the fridge."

Shelby laughed. "I agree. He can be a very naughty little monkey."

"Chester doesn't mean to be bad." Emily's expression turned all serious. "He just can't help it sometimes. Especially when he's scared."

"That's right. So, are you still scared? Will you be jumping on the bed and stealing pudding?"

Emily wrapped her arms around Shelby's neck and grinned. "No. I'm going to get better. Like you did."

"Good plan." Shelby returned her hug.

Nick closed his eyes and blew out a long breath. Shelby saved the day. She'd said just the right things and pulled Emily out of her funk.

Shelby was right, he did owe her—big time. For more than she knew.

He sucked.

4

"Getting all dressed up and wearing stiff shoes is annoying . . . especially for bored monkeys."
Chester Goes to a Wedding

Shelby drew in the subtle scent of Nick's sensual cologne as he drove her home from the hospital in his equally sexy Porsche. It made her miss the one she used to own. Her Prius was nowhere near as fun to drive.

Staring out the window, she still couldn't figure why she'd shared her past with him. Was it the way he'd held her hand so tightly, steadying her, and the way his whole face softened when he smiled at her? No man had ever looked at her like that before. Certainly no one like Nick. Hopefully she'd see the same gleam in Greg's eyes when she saw him soon.

Just to be sure she wasn't sending Nick mixed signals, because they were pretty darned mixed-up in her own head, she added a dose of snark to her tone and said, "You do realize if everyone drove a car like this, your children won't have clean air to breathe, Nick."

"I'm never having kids, so I figure I can use up more than my fair share."

"I don't believe you. Not after seeing the way you are with Emily. She adores you and vice versa."

He scowled as he stared at the road ahead. "I make it a policy to tell the truth. And after watching my father devastate my mom when I was a kid, I swore I'd never marry."

"Oaths made when we're children don't count."

"Speaking of kids, why would a seven-year-old miss dinner and then have to make her own grilled cheese?"

She turned and looked at him. Concern etched his features. Just like it had at the hospital when he'd led her to the chair she'd so badly needed during her almost-fainting moment. But after meeting Nick's mom, a tall, dark-haired, beautiful and caring woman, she wasn't sure Nick could understand.

"My mom and dad were loving people, but they sucked at being parents. That thing called responsibility eluded them." She blew out a long breath and faced straight ahead. Maybe it'd make it easier to explain if she didn't look at him. "My mom got herself pregnant by the gardener at seventeen. When she married my low-class father she was disinherited by her family. My parents liked to party and often passed out before my sister and I got fed." She glanced his way again. "We ate a lot of yogurt."

Nick frowned as he switched gears. "It was your parents' job to keep you safe. And they failed. That fire wasn't your fault, it was an accident."

She laughed bitterly. "That sounds good in theory. But if I hadn't used the stove after I was told specifically not to because the knob was tricky, I'd still have my family."

Her cell rang, saving her from the rest of the painful conversation she didn't want to have. The screen showed it was her aunt.

"I have to take this." She drew a deep breath, digging deep for patience. "Hello, Aunt Victoria. How are you?"

"I have a disaster on my hands. You need to help."

If her aunt tried to set her up with one more of her pompous, rich friends' sons, she'd go mad. She couldn't wait until Greg got back and she won him over. Maybe then her aunt would leave her alone. "What do you need?"

"I'm sponsoring a black-tie charity event at the club on Saturday, and the celebrity backed out. Imagine my surprise when some of the ladies talking about replacements mentioned an up-and-coming local author, and it was you! They said your little children's books have become quite popular and they'd love to have you."

"Imagine that." Shelby didn't bother to disguise her sarcasm.

"You'll need to be at the club at seven. It's formal so you'll wear a long gown and we won't have to work around your legs. I know you must be struggling since you left the business, but please don't show up in something from last season. It'd reflect poorly on the family. Just this once, you may charge my account at any of my usual shops. Oh, and if you don't have a date I can arrange—"

"No! I'm good." Shelby's jaw clenched. "And I can afford a new dress. I'm not a pauper just because I don't work for Uncle Jack anymore."

Her aunt sniffed. "Please don't take that tone with me, Shelby. I was trying to be helpful. And don't be late." Then she hung up.

Shelby tossed the phone into her purse and crossed her arms. Dammit. Now she was going to have to spend money on a new dress she'd probably never wear again on top of springing for a tux for her date.

Nick cleared his throat. "Problem?"

"I have to make a command performance at my aunt and uncle's club Saturday night. The snooty Bay View, which is a stupid name because there aren't any bays in Denver. Should be a scintillating evening."

"My dad belongs to that one too. Only the best for him."

Shelby rolled her eyes. "Same with my aunt and uncle." But who should she ask to accompany her? Someone who'd shock her aunt and uncle could be fun. Maybe she'd ask her friend Mike. He was a tattoo artist. It'd drive Uncle Jack insane.

But poor Mike would be bored out of his skull. No, she liked him too much for that.

Then it hit her. Nick was a slick guy who dressed to impress. And he still owed her a favor. "Do you own a tux?"

He eyed her warily. "Yes. Why?"

"Then you're my date because you owe me."

"I thought you didn't date clients?"

"It won't be a real date, so it doesn't count."

"No way." Nick shook his head. "I hate wearing the monkey suit. Just hit me with your bat and let's call it even."

"You said if I went to the hospital, I get a free swing. So I get the swing *and* a favor. But, if you go with me, I promise I won't hit you on the head."

"Name anything else. I hate the country club set. My ass of a father might be at that party, and I don't want to run into him."

"If you say yes, I'll sweeten the pot by throwing in a stuffed Chester doll that's not coming out until next month. Emily will be the most envied kid in her class."

Emily was clearly Nick's weakness. She counted in her mind while he contemplated. *Four, three, two—*

"Oh, all right." He scowled as he pulled into her drive. "Do women come out of the womb knowing how to blackmail? You're worse than my sisters."

She grinned at her victory. "Pick me up at six thirty and don't be late or I'll sic my aunt on you. You're just her type."

⁂

Just to annoy Shelby for making him wear his tux, Nick showed up on Saturday night at six ten. Women hated when their dates arrived early and paced.

He didn't even care that his tie didn't look right because that'd irritate her too. She was cute when she was mad at him.

While tugging at his overly starched collar, he made his way up Shelby's front path. When the door swung open, his mouth went dry.

Shelby stood before him in the sexiest red dress he'd ever seen. She had more cleavage than he'd realized and curves aplenty.

"Good, you're early. Let's go." Shelby grabbed her purse and shut the door behind her.

He'd been tempted to let her open her own car door in retaliation for making him risk seeing his father, but he just couldn't do it. Instinct took over and he beat her to the handle. As he swung the door open wide, Shelby stopped and frowned.

"You really suck at tying bow ties. Here, let me." She threw her sparkly little purse into the car and then fixed his tie in under thirty seconds. "That's better. Although you probably did that just to annoy me."

He checked out her amazing rear end while she maneuvered herself into his low car. Damn she was hot. But totally off-limits. She wasn't the sex-with-no-strings type.

He slid behind the wheel and backed out. He'd known plenty of beautiful women, but what was it about Shelby that made him want to know more? It threw him off-balance.

But he still wasn't happy about the tux. "Just to be clear, if it's not an open bar, you're buying the drinks tonight, Shelby."

She pulled down the visor and flipped open the lit mirror. It was torture watching her swipe shiny gloss onto her full lips before she gave them a smack.

"A Marx never throws an event in which one would have to pay for alcohol. That would just be *déclassé* Nicolas."

Her rich-bitch imitation drew a chuckle from him.

Damn. He honestly liked her. Originally, he was just going to study her setup, extract key marketing, client, and sales info, and then disappear. But maybe she didn't have to find out what he was up to. Especially if he played along so she thought he was really trying. He'd just make sure she went along on his dates using her little Bluetooth thing and he'd pretend to be clueless. He really didn't want to hurt her, just save his stubborn sister who wouldn't let him help keep her business in the black.

He asked, "So, what's the plan tonight? Do the minimum and then slip out early?"

Shelby sighed. "That's always my hope for one of my aunt's fundraisers. But if it goes on too late, you can leave. I can always catch a ride home in my aunt and uncle's limo."

"I'm not going to ditch you, Shelby. *That* would be déclassé."

When she laughed, her smile sparked an answering grin from him. Maybe they'd actually have a good time, even if his father was bound to be there.

As they drove in silence, he caught Shelby staring at him. "What? Did I cut myself shaving or something?" He ran a hand down the side of his face to check.

"No. I just can't figure you out. Why would a guy like you need my help? Let's face it: you're not ugly, you have a hot car, and I know from your address you live in one of the most exclusive subdivisions in Denver. You're kind of arrogant sometimes, but then, some women actually like that. So what's the deal?"

Crap! Had she guessed he was spying on her? But he wasn't arrogant. Maybe he'd taken his bad-client act a little too far.

Failing to come up with a good retort, he shrugged. "Maybe I just wanted to try something new?" That was lame. He needed to step it up quick or Grandma was going to haunt him for the rest of his life.

Her eyes narrowed. "So you were completely honest on your questionnaire? That's really the kind of woman you think you want?"

"Yes. I think I'd enjoy spending time with a woman like that."

An accident on the freeway ahead had him downshifting. That's all he needed. To be stuck in traffic with Shelby interrogating him. When they came to a dead stop, he turned and faced her. "Why is it so wrong to want the woman I described?"

"I've never had a client say they aren't looking for love or a real relationship before. It's why people use my service."

Fail there. He should've kept his mouth shut about that. "I'm hoping you can find me that woman so we could have a nice time and enjoy each other's company until it fizzles out. Not everyone wants to be married and have kids . . . like you obviously do."

"Leave me out of this. We're analyzing you. Do you have any women friends?"

"No. But none of my other guy friends do either. So what?"

"You'd really rather have a girlfriend who likes sports over one with say, intelligence and wit?"

"Intelligence and wit would be a nice bonus. I just hate it when women pretend to like sports when I first meet them, and then get mad because I spend too much time watching football with the guys."

"So, you prefer to hang out with men over being with a woman?"

"Yeah, especially during football season."

"You do realize the woman you described on your questionnaire is basically a guy, but with girl parts, right?"

"What are you trying to say, Shelby?"

The traffic started moving again, so he put the car in gear and gave it some gas.

She ignored his question. "You mentioned you didn't want to run into your dad tonight, so you seem to have father issues too."

"Father issues? I think it's perfectly normal to dislike a cheating bastard."

"Maybe you've come to me because you're having trouble facing the truth?"

"About what?"

"Think about it Nick. You prefer to hang with guys, and you can't commit to women. Maybe you'd rather be with a man?"

What!

"Shelby, I'm not—"

She wrapped her arms around her waist and laughed out loud. "The look on your face, Nick . . ." She had to stop and catch her breath, she was laughing so hard. "Priceless."

"Cute. How are you the top-rated matchmaker in town if you tease your clients like that?"

She sobered up quickly and crossed her arms. "I don't tease my other clients. Guys like you just bring it out in me, I guess."

"Guys like me? What does that mean?"

She shrugged and looked out the window. "Never mind. It doesn't matter. Maybe you and I shouldn't work together."

He'd played the jerk card a little too well when they'd first met to test her. So now he needed to show her he wasn't arrogant and that he truly respected her so she wouldn't dump him. "Maybe you tease me because you actually like me. Have you ever considered that?"

Now it was *her* expression that made *him* laugh. "You don't have to look so horrified, Shelby. Maybe I'm not the guy you think I am. Why don't we call a truce and just get through tonight before we go tearing up contracts? Deal?" He held out his fist for a friendly bump.

"Really?" She frowned at his fist. "We're going to fist bump, like men? Maybe this is why you can't find the right woman." She rolled her eyes, but fist bumped him anyway. "Okay. Your first assignment is to try to act like a gentleman tonight. No burping, scratching, or anything Neanderthal-like. Got it?"

"Got it." Relief rushed through him. That had been too close a call. He still needed to figure out how she ran her business and couldn't afford to screw up again. Luckily, his mother hadn't raised an ape. After his father left, his mother never missed an opportunity to point out how to treat a lady.

Shelby pulled out her phone, ignoring him the rest of the way to the club. Clearly she still didn't like him enough to make the effort at simple small talk, even though he was doing her a favor. He'd just have to show Shelby Marx how wrong she was about "guys like him."

The accident on the freeway delayed them, but because he'd been early, they arrived at the party only a few minutes late. Nick gave the valet his keys, then slipped his hand around Shelby's slender waist and led her up the steps of Denver's most exclusive country club. Maybe if things went well, he might even be able to snag a few new, rich clients. Could be a productive evening.

When they entered the ballroom, an elderly man dressed in a black suit with the country club's crest on the pocket smiled at Shelby. "Good evening, Ms. Marx. Your aunt and uncle await your arrival at the front of the ballroom. May I show you the way?"

Shelby leaned up on her tiptoes and kissed the man's cheek. "Nice to see you, Arthur. This is my . . . date, Nick."

Arthur tilted his head. "A pleasure, sir."

Shelby's date? Not her escort or companion? Maybe he was growing on her already.

As Arthur led them through the opulent ballroom, weaving around small groups of Denver's elite, Shelby whispered, "My uncle can be a bit . . . intimidating. And my aunt? Well, you'll see for yourself. Don't let them get to you."

He threw his arm around her shoulder. "I'm not easily intimidated, Shelby. Relax."

As they approached the raised dais in the front of the ballroom, he spotted the man who'd broken his mother's heart, and pulled up short.

Shelby glanced up at him. "What?"

"That's my father over there, talking to the bimbo who's obviously had one too many plastic surgeries. Not surprising, that's his type."

Shelby laughed as she tucked her arm through his and pulled him forward. "Well, since that bimbo is my aunt Victoria, we should probably join them."

Great. That wasn't going to help get rid of her urge to dump him from her client list.

"Sorry. I was commenting on my father—"

Ignoring his babbling explanation she said, "No, you're right. My aunt has had one too many procedures. But after the few cryptic things you've said about your father, I'm curious to meet him."

Shelby tugged him closer to his father, a top divorce lawyer—a destroyer of families. These people were his type of clients. Of course he'd not want to miss an opportunity to pick up some new business.

It could be a long night.

When they joined them, Shelby's aunt turned her overly botoxed face their way and said, "You're late, dear." Only her tone betrayed her annoyance. Her face was so shot up with poison, not a muscle moved.

"Accident on I-25," Shelby replied and then pushed Nick closer. "And this is your companion's son, Nick Caldwell."

When her aunt's eyes lit with pleasure, his stomach took a dive.

"I see Shelby's taste in men has finally improved. You look just like your handsome father, Nick. Pleasure to meet you."

He hated when women who refused to accept their fading beauty looked at him like he was the last éclair in the box. Let her beam that scary smile at someone her own age, like his dad.

Steeling himself, he held out his hand to receive her handshake. "Nice to meet you, Mrs. Marx." Then he lowered his hand to his side and greeted his father. "Dad. This is Shelby."

His father said, "Hello, Son," but couldn't seem to take his eyes off of Shelby. His father's gaze ran up and down the length of Shelby's tight, low-cut dress. "A delight to meet you,

Shelby. Are all the Marx women as beautiful as you and your aunt?"

Shelby reached out and shook his father's hand, then it looked as though his father was going to pull her hand to his mouth for a kiss.

Frickin' pervert!

He'd never know for sure because Shelby's hand quickly slid from his grasp and she said, "What a charming thing to say. It's nice to meet you, Mr. Caldwell."

He'd forgotten Shelby had grown up around people like his dad. He admired the way she politely blew him off. Or, maybe his father had released her hand.

Didn't matter, his father was a jerk either way and needed to understand Shelby was off-limits. He wrapped his hand around her waist, pulling Shelby closer in a silent back-off gesture.

Aunt Victoria said, "Shelby is one of the many items being auctioned off this evening, Edward. Pay enough for the privilege and you'll be able to accompany her on a date."

Nick and Shelby both said "What?" in unison.

Shelby slammed her hands on her curvy little hips and faced her aunt. "You didn't say anything about auctioning me off!"

"Surely I mentioned that part, Shelby. You must not have been listening again." Auntie Botox turned her wicked gaze toward his father and smiled. "If you'll excuse us Edward, Shelby and I need to powder our noses."

Aunt Victoria's clawlike hand wrapped around Shelby's arm as she none so gently dragged her niece toward the exit. "I'll have her back in a jiffy, Nick."

He turned to his father who was watching the ladies cross the ballroom. Was his father admiring Shelby's ass?

Admittedly it was hard not to notice Shelby's nicely rounded feature in that dress. Or maybe his dad had his eye on Aunt Victoria's? He hoped to God his father wasn't banging married women again like before. He thought that had stopped after his father divorced his mom and then moved on to much younger prey.

Just as he leaned close to tell his father to forget about bidding on Shelby, someone slapped his father on the back. "Edward. It's been ages. How are you?"

His father shook the man's hand. "Nice to see you, Jack." Then he held a hand in Nick's direction. "This is your niece's date, my son, Nick."

Jack's eyes narrowed as he shook Nick's hand. It looked like Shelby's uncle had been under the knife more than once as well. The Marx's plastic surgeon had to be one wealthy doctor by now.

"Shelby's date, huh? Good thing you're Edward's son, or I'd have to give you the third degree. But I'll warn you, I've yet to meet a man good enough for my Shelby."

Nick couldn't resist defending himself and Shelby too, for that matter. Her aunt and uncle were unbearable. "Then it's fortunate we've finally met."

⚜

Shelby finished off her second glass of wine with dinner. She was due to be auctioned off any minute and needed all the courage she could ingest. Damn her aunt for tricking her. What if no one bid on her?

Worse, what if she didn't turn out to be worth more than that hideous painting someone donated?

Mortifying.

Nick refilled her empty wine glass. "Stop fidgeting, Shelby. You'll be the hit of the auction."

"You're loving every minute of this, aren't you?"

"Yup." He chuckled before whispering in her ear, "You bribed me into being your date knowing I'd suffer for it, but I'm the one having all the fun. It's *so* unfair."

Ignoring his sarcastic remark, she took a deep drink from her wineglass. Nick was ridiculously gorgeous in his tux, so it had been no surprise when women of all ages flirted with him—including disgusting overtures from her aunt—but Nick never took the bait.

She reluctantly gave him points for that. As handsome as Nick was, he didn't seem to use it to his advantage. Except for when he helped out her shy client, but that had been for a good cause.

All evening, she'd tried to ignore him for the most part, but he'd been well versed on every subject, politely chatted with everyone she introduced him to, and only left her side to get their drinks. It confused her. He wasn't at all like he'd been at the café.

Nick's big shoulder gently bumped hers. "So, what made you pick Summer Sinclair for your pen name?"

She glanced at their tablemates to be sure no one was listening. "I was born with it."

His right brow zinged up. "You changed your name?"

"My aunt said she wouldn't take me in unless I changed it and became a Marx. She thought Summer Sinclair sounded like a porn star's name."

He laughed. "It must really chap her ass you're using it as your pen name then, huh?"

"That was the plan." Taking another long drink from her wineglass, she smiled, reveling in her small dose of revenge.

"Nice move, Shelby." Nick chuckled as he leaned closer and studied the program. "It says here whoever wins the pleasure of your company gets to choose one of three venues."

"Let me see that." She snatched the program from his hand and scanned the list of choices. One was lunch at an upscale restaurant, the other a dinner at an intimate bed-and-breakfast, and the third was for a party in a luxury executive suite to watch the Denver Broncos play on Monday night. Her uncle was the one who donated his box for the game.

Nick tugged the paper back from her. "Most women wouldn't consider a football game a fun date. Why would they offer that for you?"

"The person's place I'm taking in the auction is a retired Denver Bronco player. I imagine it was their way of encouraging the men to bid as well."

"Maybe you'll get lucky and one of those fictional knights you're waiting for will win and pick the cozy bed-and-breakfast. That way, you'd only have to go upstairs to get even luckier."

"Funny. But just like you don't do real relationships, I don't do one-night stands." She finished off her wine. "Besides, most men need a little time to work up to the sight of my legs."

Why had she just told him that? Probably the wine's fault. She'd better quit drinking before she did something really stupid.

She saw rather than felt Nick's big hand pat her knee. "I'm sure your legs don't look as bad as you think, Shelby. Besides, you have many more interesting body parts. That dress is doing a fine job displaying them tonight."

She could have kissed him for that. If he'd been anyone other than Nick Caldwell, she would have. "Yeah, well I don't look as good as you do in that tux. But then, you already knew that I'm sure."

"You're slipping, Shelby. That sounded dangerously close to a compliment."

Before she could finish their sparring match, her aunt's voice over the speakers asked Shelby to join her on stage. "Well, this is it. See you on the other side." She slapped her beaded purse into his belly. "Guard this with your life."

Shelby stood and threw her shoulders back, plastering on a smile as she made her way to the podium. If she was going to be displayed like a piece of meat, she'd be filet mignon. She'd never give her aunt the satisfaction of seeing her sweat.

Her uncle Jack was a pain in the butt with his protectiveness, but at least he was nice to her. Her aunt Victoria had never wanted children and had resented that her uncle insisted Shelby live with them.

Careful to lift her dress as little as possible while ascending the stairs, so as not to expose her legs to everyone, she took her place beside her aunt.

Please don't let me pass out. Or puke up all that wine.

Aunt Victoria plastered on one of her fake smiles for the crowd. "As some of you may know, we were supposed to have the handsome and dashing Michael Reading with us here tonight. Every woman's dream date and every man's best friend. Unfortunately for us, he's shooting a commercial overseas and was unable to make it at the last minute."

Shelby closed her eyes, suppressing a moan. She'd look like ground beef after her aunt's glimmering introduction for the man she wasn't.

"As a last resort my niece was available to step in. Shelby writes children's books as one of her many little hobbies. Some of you may better know her by her pen name, Summer Sinclair?"

Many little hobbies? She could choke her aunt.

Matching Mr. Right

When Shelby met Nick's gaze, he shook his head and then joined in with everyone else and clapped.

Wait. They were clapping for her?

The loud applause, mostly from the women in the audience, had her aunt blinking in surprise. "Oh, thank you for being so understanding. The venues were obviously chosen with Michael in mind, but if you win, you may bring up to two children along as well. So, let's get the bidding started. Remember, the proceeds will benefit our wonderful charities."

Shelby held her breath as the first bid flew out from the back of the ballroom. Squinting against the bright lights, Shelby made out an older woman holding up her auction paddle. "Five hundred dollars."

Mostly female voices called out as the bid grew to a thousand, then slowly built to thirty-five hundred. She'd beat out the crap painting, so it wasn't a complete bust.

"Four thousand!" The call came from Nick's dad.

Shelby's stomach dropped.

Panic shot through her as she searched for Nick. His seat was empty. Did he ditch her after all? If she had to go on a date with his father she'd definitely hit Nick over the head with her bat. Hopefully he'd just gone to the restroom and would get back in time to save her. Nick mentioned his father liked to date younger women. Maybe she was too old for him?

No, his dad hadn't made any moves on her earlier. He was a complete gentleman. But either way, it'd be too uncomfortable to fathom.

Then a lady in the front bid forty-one hundred and Shelby's heart rate slowed a bit.

Thank God.

Shelby's aunt called out, "Going once, going twice—"

Nick's father interrupted with, "Five thousand!"

Applause roared from the crowd as Shelby desperately searched the back of the room for Nick.

Her aunt said, "The bid is five thousand. Going once, going twice . . . sold! Congratulations Edward. Now what venue will you choose?"

Sweat slid down Shelby's spine. From Nick's description of his father, she feared she knew what a man like him would choose. The bed-and-breakfast. Yikes!

Nick finally reappeared holding his cell phone. He had a suspicious bulge in his suit coat that had to be her purse. Confusion creased his brow as he spoke to one of their tablemates. Then he turned and scowled at his father.

Nick's father said, "You'll have to ask Shelby's date, my son, Nick. I bid on Shelby for him. I thought they'd enjoy an all-expenses-paid outing."

Nick's expression turned thunderous before he turned his back on his father and stormed out of the ballroom, leaving her standing up front like the last kid on the playground waiting to be picked for dodgeball. What had Nick's father said to make him so angry? It didn't make any sense.

Or was it because she wasn't Nick's usual type? Tall, blonde, and built like a Barbie. Humiliated to be left standing on the stage, all eyes on her, while her so-called date dumped her, her blood boiled with rage.

She was going to kill Nick Caldwell.

5

> "Throwing things while arguing is wrong. But it sure makes a mad monkey feel better."
> *Chester's Big Fight*

Nick spotted Shelby walking toward the country club's front doors, flanked by her aunt and uncle. Picking up the pace, he slipped his hand around her arm and stopped her. "There you are, Shelby. Ready to go?"

She sent him a deep scowl, but before she could let him have it, her aunt said, "She's ready."

When Shelby's uncle opened his mouth to protest, Victoria sent him a pointed look and then grabbed his arm and tugged him toward the door. "We had no desire to add another hour to our drive, so thank you, Nick. Good night."

Shelby huffed out a breath and crossed her arms as she stared at their retreating backs.

Figuring it best to remain silent, Nick walked beside her as they descended the front steps.

He greeted the attendant and slipped him a twenty along with his valet ticket. "Make it quick."

The kid nodded and jogged away.

When he reached out to comfort Shelby, she stepped away.

After his Porsche arrived, he opened the door for her then rounded the car and slid behind the wheel. He grabbed her little purse from his coat pocket and laid it on her lap. "So what is so important in there that I had to guard it with my life?"

"Lipstick. And cab fare. It looked like I was going to need it for a moment there." She huffed out a breath and stared straight ahead. "Not only did you say you wouldn't ditch me, but then you did it in front of everyone, Nick!"

He hadn't meant to abandon her up on stage like that. Before he could find the right place to start his apology, she said, "It's no wonder your girlfriend dumped you last month. You're mean. I realize I'm not your type, but you didn't have to make it look like you'd rather take a bullet than go out with *me!*"

"I wanted to go out with you, but you said you don't date clients. And Beth wasn't really my girlfriend. She was a . . . sex partner. I didn't date her I just . . ."

"Screwed her? Nice, Nick. Why would I have expected anything more from you?"

"Really? I don't see you going on any dates either, miss I'm-waiting-for-my-fairytale-prince!"

Her tiny purse bounced off his shoulder. "Greg's not a fairytale. He'll be back in the country on Wednesday!"

"Who the hell is Greg?" He tucked her purse back into his pocket for safety purposes, and started the car. They were holding up the valet line, so he put the car in gear and peeled out toward the exit.

When she remained silent he debated letting her stew for a while, but his conscience got the better of him. "My father must've asked Emily, who isn't old enough to see what a jerk he is and adores him, to call me away. That's why I left, to talk to her. But there was no emergency, so I came back inside. That's when I realized my dad had bid on you."

Shelby cranked up the radio full blast and then turned her chin toward her window.

Unfortunately for her, she was a captive audience and she'd damned well listen.

He hit the mute button. "I didn't mean to abandon you up there. I was afraid I'd deck my father if I didn't leave. He did that in front of everyone to make it look like he's the father-of-the-year instead of the ass he truly is."

Shelby murmured, "He couldn't be worse than my aunt Victoria."

Nick merged into the southbound traffic on the freeway, settling in for the ride.

He'd never discussed what his father had done with anyone outside of his family, but after seeing how Shelby's family treated her, maybe she'd understand.

"When I was ten, I was playing baseball in the street at my friend's house when I saw my dad's car pull up down the block. When the game was over I thought I'd see if I could catch a ride home with him. The short version is I caught him with his pants around his ankles doing the lady of the house. I found out later he'd visited a few other grateful, lonely women after he'd helped bleed their ex-husbands dry."

"You saw something like that when you were ten?" Shelby slipped her hand over his on the console and gave it a gentle squeeze.

Her show of support encouraged him to continue. "My dad yelled at me and then told me to wait in the car. On the drive home he said I'd only hurt my mother by telling her what I'd seen. He asked me to lie, and tell her he'd found me walking home and picked me up. He swore it'd never happen again. The next day he bought me a new mountain bike I'd had my eye on."

Shelby grunted. "Okay, you win. He's worse than my aunt."

Nodding he said, "So, I decided I'd keep my mouth shut, but every time I rode that damned bike I felt like a heel. I love my mom and I hated him for making me keep his secret. About three weeks later, I went into his study to find a pen. He sat in his big leather chair with his back to the door, talking on the phone, so he didn't notice I was there. When I realized he was making a date to meet a woman at a hotel, I lost it. I screamed at him at the top of my lungs. When my mom came to see what was wrong, I told her everything." Swallowing back the bile rising in his throat he said, "They divorced soon after. I helped destroy my family."

"And that's why you never lie? Because of your dad?" Shelby frowned. "Not a bad trait, but your mom would have found out eventually, Nick, even if you hadn't told her. It wasn't your fault, and it wasn't your problem to fix. It was between your mom and dad."

"If I hadn't said anything, there wouldn't have been anything to fix." He shook his head as he exited the freeway, regretting he had to let go of her hand to switch gears. "She probably felt like she had to kick him out after I exposed him, to show my sisters it wasn't right to let a man treat them that way. Worse, what if she knew, but not having any way to support us, pretended not to know until she could stash enough money away to leave him? If I'd kept my mouth shut, my mom would have been so much better off financially now. He's a divorce attorney, for God's sake. My mom only gets whatever crumbs he throws her way while he lives in a mansion and belongs to clubs like the Bay View. That's on *my* head."

"You told me the other day the fire wasn't my fault and as much as you believe that, I believe you're not responsible for the destruction of your family. Your father is. But that won't change the way you feel any more than it did when you said the same to me. We're both still wallowing in guilt and too damn stubborn to forgive ourselves."

"Maybe. But I *am* sorry about tonight."

His cell vibrated as they approached Shelby's house. Snagging it from his jacket, he glanced at the screen. When he saw it was Beth, he ignored the text and tossed the phone on the console.

Shelby smirked. "It's late. Booty call perhaps?"

"Don't know." Maybe Beth had changed her mind about their arrangement. Strangely, he had no desire to be with her anymore.

As he turned into Shelby's driveway, his phone slid off the console and onto Shelby's lap.

She picked it up. "Sorry, but I couldn't help notice the screen. Whoever *Naughtylawyer* is says to hurry home. She wants you." Shelby arched a brow. "I'm assuming this is from the sex partner you claim you're broken up with who's waiting at home for you? So, your real plan was to keep that woman on the side while I set you up on dates? If that's the case, then we need to terminate our contract." She handed his phone back. "And you say you never lie."

Beth had some seriously bad timing.

"Beth is my ex . . . partner . . . but she's still my neighbor. That's what she meant about hurry home. She's been so busy with work I haven't even seen her since she broke up with me a month ago, Shelby. I swear."

Shelby opened her door and swung her legs out of the car, giving him her back. "Whatever. I don't think I'm the right one to find you a match anyway. I'll reverse the payment you sent. And now your other debt to me has been paid, so have a nice life."

"We have a contract. I'd prefer you to live up to your end of the bargain. And I told them to have the limo pick me up first. We should be here about five thirty for the game on Monday."

Shelby froze in her efforts to exit the car and then turned and faced him. "*We're* going on the date? Not you and the naughty lawyer? And you chose the football game?"

"I love football." He tossed the purse her way. "Don't forget your lipstick."

Shelby's snag would make an outfielder proud. "What if I didn't like football, you arrogant jerk? You have *so* much to learn about women." She slammed the door.

He stuck his head out the window as Shelby stomped to her front door. "Good thing I have you to teach me. So, was that a yes to the game? We could make it a lesson if you'd like."

She muttered under her breath as she unlocked her front door. Once she got it open she called out, "Only if you bring Emily along—if she's feeling up to it. Then I'd be sure to have a ride home. You'd never ditch her!"

When her front door slammed shut, he smiled. Good idea. Emily seemed almost back to herself when he'd seen her earlier. It'd be harder for Shelby to stay mad at him when there was a cute kid like Em around.

As he backed out of Shelby's driveway, a thought struck him. She never answered his question. Who the hell was Greg?

※

Shelby flung her purse onto the couch and then leaned down to rip off her arch-maiming heels. Tossing her shoes in the general direction of her bedroom, she lifted the front of her long dress and made a beeline toward the kitchen. She needed ice cream, if there was any left. She'd never eaten as much ice cream as she had since meeting Nick earlier in the week. He had to be the most infuriating man on earth.

She yanked the freezer door open and grinned. Jo had gone shopping. God bless her.

Mint chocolate chip or Rocky Road? Decisions, decisions.

Grabbing both, she snatched up a spoon and then plopped down in the nook. The combination of both flavors in one bite was oddly delicious.

Jo stumbled into the kitchen, yawning as she ran her hands through her tousled hair. She found a spoon and then sat across from Shelby. As was their habit, Jo held out her spoon for an ice cream toast. After Shelby tapped spoons with her, Jo sampled a mixed bite like Shelby's.

Jo winced. "That's just gross." She shivered in disgust as she pulled the Rocky Road toward her. "Door slamming and ice cream? Must've been some night."

Shelby took a big bite and cringed as brain freeze incapacitated her for moment. When her powers of speech returned, she told Jo about her evening.

Jo listened intently as the ice cream in it's cardboard box steadily disappeared. When Shelby finally got to the front-door-slamming part, Jo frowned. "If he's such an arrogant jerk, why are you going to the game with him on Monday?"

Shelby sighed and put the lid back on her container before she made herself sick. "When have I ever missed a Broncos home game? Besides, I would've run into him anyway because Uncle Jack donated our executive suite for the auction."

"Ah." Jo nodded as her face lit with an evil grin. "It'll be fun to see the look on his face when he shows up and sees you dressed in full Broncos regalia. The joke's going to be on him."

Shelby chuckled. "It'll be even better when we get to the box and he sees who else is there."

"Could be a Chester book in the making."

"You never know. Sorry I woke you." Shelby stood and put the ice cream away. "'Nite."

As Shelby gathered up her dress and headed toward her bedroom, Jo said, "So, do you still want to come to Greg's welcome-home party on Wednesday, or will you be busy with Mr. Arrogant?"

Shelby pulled up short. "Of course I want to come. I've got my, 'look, I'm really a girl' outfit all picked out. Why would you even ask?"

Jo shrugged before she put their spoons into the dishwasher. "I've never seen a man get such a big reaction from you. Normally, you'd just blow off a guy like Nick."

"Believe me, the last person I'd ever want to date is Nick. I've never met anyone who gets under my skin like he can!"

"My point, exactly." Jo turned off the light.

⁂

Nick headed for home. Watching the game on Monday from an executive suite with all the food and beer he wanted would be awesome. It even included a limo so he wouldn't have to worry about having a few drinks and then driving. And he'd get to see Shelby again.

Thanks dear old dad. You bastard!

As Nick pulled into his driveway, visions of a pair of sweats and a cold beer filled his head. What a crapper of a night.

Just as the garage door rumbled closed behind him, his doorbell peeled. Must be Beth.

He swung his front door open and found blonde, beautiful Beth standing before him in her skimpy robe. "Hey, there." Beth in her see-through robe couldn't hold a candle to Shelby in her red dress.

"You're wearing a tux?" Beth's eyes grew wide. "Yum."

She slapped the door shut behind her, pressed her lush body against his and kissed him. He quickly broke the kiss, suddenly realizing how badly it was Shelby's full lips he'd like to taste.

He grasped Beth's wrists to stop her busy fingers from trying to unbutton his shirt. "I thought we were going our separate ways."

She smiled. "I made a mistake. I miss you, Nick."

His sister's words about Beth staying away so he'd miss her clanged in his head. Crap.

He took her hand and led her to the couch, gently nudging her onto it. "When we were together, we never spent the entire night, and we didn't go to dinners or movies, so we wouldn't get attached. Right?"

"Well, yeah. But . . . don't you miss me at all, Nick?" When Beth's eyes misted with tears, his stomach took a dive. His sister had been right. And did that mean she was right about the other thing too? The part about Beth being in love with him?

He ran a hand through his hair, searching for the right words. "Of course I miss you, Beth. As a friend, absolutely. But I told you from the beginning I couldn't give you anything more than friendship."

Beth closed her eyes and her shoulders slumped. "I know that in my head, but my heart thinks otherwise. You'd be a great husband and father, Nick. Something tells me it's just going to take the right woman to make you see that." She opened her eyes and stared deeply into his for a moment before shaking her head. "But I'm not that woman. Am I?"

A stab of guilt arrowed straight to his gut. She wasn't and never would be, but that didn't mean he wanted to hurt her.

"They're my issues, not yours, that make it impossible to be together long-term, Beth. You are an incredible woman and deserve more than I can give you."

She slowly stood as a single tear ran down her cheek.

He wanted to ease her pain, but it'd be best to let her go. Any encouragement he gave would give her the wrong idea.

Beth wiped her cheek and worked up a smile. "Well, then it looks like it's time for both of us to get back out there and quit taking the easy road." She wrapped her arms around his neck and whispered, "But I still want to peel you out of that tux, Nick. How about it? One last time?"

After a month without sex, it killed him, but he couldn't. Not when they had to end things. And not when a certain sexy little blonde with killer green eyes kept popping into his thoughts at the most annoying moments. "It'd just make this harder. I want to part as friends." He took her hand and led her to the door.

She forced a sad smile. "We'll always be friends, Nick. If you change your mind, I'm right down the street. 'Nite."

She gave him a soft kiss on the cheek then walked toward her house.

He waited until she was inside, then closed his door. Something in his gut told him that had been way too easy. Especially if the "L" word had been involved.

Beth just needed to find the right guy, and then she'd be fine. First thing in the morning, assuming Shelby had cooled off enough to talk to him, he'd find that for Beth. And by throwing another client Shelby's way, maybe she'd forgive him for abandoning her on stage.

Problem solved.

6

> "Chester liked to tease girls and pull their hair because he secretly liked them. But that can get a monkey into big trouble."
> *Chester's Very Long Timeout*

Shelby paused the yoga workout playing on her television to answer the doorbell. It was probably Jo's mom stopping by on her way home from church to lecture them because they'd skipped.

After wiping the sweat from her face with a towel, she peered through the peephole.

Not again.

Nick wore nicely fitted jeans along with a chambray shirt, his sleeves rolled twice to expose his muscular forearms. It was the first time she'd seen him in casual clothes. He wore them just as well as a suit.

She opened the door and stuck just her head out, leaving her shorts-clad legs hidden. "Someone else in the hospital? Or did you come to apologize for your lame behavior last night?"

"I said I was sorry." He shot her a typical Nick grin. "And now I have a dating emergency."

"What? All the women you've scorned plotting against you?"

He quirked a brow. "Talking to clients that way won't keep you in business long."

"Ditching me in front of everyone won't keep you as my client very long either, pal. I'll call you later. I'm busy." She started to close the wooden door but he opened the glass storm door and stuck his big tennis shoe inside.

"There's another full fee in it for you. It's Beth."

That got her attention. Her Visa bill was due. "The ex-sex partner? Why isn't she here instead of you?"

"Let me in and I'll tell you." Nick pushed on the door.

"Stop! I'm not . . . dressed."

"You're naked behind there?" His grin turned wicked.

Shelby leaned her shoulder a little further to the side to prove to the pervert she had clothes on. "No, I've been working out and I'm all sweaty."

"I like a hot, sweaty woman." He raised his hand to push the door open.

She pressed her hand to his hard chest to stop him. "Seriously, Nick. Just wait here and I'll put some pants on. Then you can tell me all about your emergency."

"Pants?" Nick's eyes narrowed. "I don't care about your legs, Shelby, if that's what this is about. All I care about is getting Beth a soul mate. And maybe some more of your chocolate chip cookies."

The pest clearly wasn't going away, so she let him in and then made a run for it. She hadn't gotten three steps before his long arms stopped her and swung her around to face him. He kept his eyes firmly on hers, never letting them wander lower.

He was probably afraid of what he'd see. Or maybe he was waiting for her permission before he looked.

His hands gently gripped her waist, anchoring her in place. "Let's get this part over with so we can get down to business. Okay?"

Her heart pounded. Why should she care what Nick thought of her legs? The repulsive view would serve him right for showing up unannounced at her house again. "Fine, but don't say I didn't warn you." She took a step back and held her breath.

Nick frowned as he studied her legs. He twirled his finger, indicating she should turn around.

"Oh, for goodness sake!" She crossed her arms and turned her back to him so he could get the full three-sixty view.

He made a choking noise. "Wow!"

Her stomach took a dive as she wrenched her chin over her shoulder. "What?"

"Your ass looks fantastic in those shorts."

Despite her disgust with him, a smile tugged at her lips. She stifled her grin as a warm wave of relief flowed through her. She'd only shown a handful of people her legs, and after the sight of them, no one had ever had the fortitude to make a joke. Why did that make her feel better instead of wanting to punch him?

She flung a hand in the direction of the couch. "Show's over, I'm going to grab a pair of sweats. Have a seat."

Nick grabbed her hand and pulled her close. "So you have some scars on your legs, Shelby. They're not off-putting, they're just there. Some of my climbing buddies who have taken bad tumbles have Frankenstein scars that make yours look tame."

"But mine are all over—"

He raised a finger to stop her. "What I hate most is the hurt you must've gone through when you lost your family and then had to endure all those surgeries alone. I'm guessing *those* scars are a lot uglier than the ones on your legs."

The breath backed up in her lungs. She hadn't expected tenderness from the caveman. Nick had surprised her once again.

She needed to leave before he saw her threatening tears. "Thanks. But it was a long time ago. Be right back."

She closed her bedroom door, shut her eyes, and drew a deep breath. Nick was right. The guilt she'd suffered while lying in those hospital beds all alone, due to her careless actions, had been almost too much to bear. She'd actually hoped she'd never wake up after each of her surgeries, and when she did, it felt like just one more punishment she'd earned for her deed.

She opened her eyes and glanced at the tall mirror standing in the corner. She hated the sight of her legs, but slowly turned to view her rear end. Did it look good in her workout shorts? She'd never thought of her butt as an asset before. Tilting her head in consideration, she smiled. Maybe it wasn't so bad after all. And maybe Nick wasn't so bad either.

After she'd dressed and pulled herself together, Shelby walked into the living room. Nick struck a Warrior Pose in front of her TV. The last time she'd let him in her house he'd used her laptop without her permission, and now he was doing her workout program? The guy was as bad as Chester. Or he had a serious case of ADD.

"What are you doing?"

He mimicked the instructor's move. "Yoga, apparently. How is this considered exercise?"

"It's not as easy as it looks." Shelby waited until Nick was standing on one foot with the other foot perched against his inner thigh and his arms stretched above his head, before she shoved him.

He landed in a heap on the carpet.

"See?" Laughing, she leaned over him for the remote. She hit the Off button just as his hands slipped around her waist. He yanked her on top of him, then rolled, pinning her under his big, hard body.

Lord, all those sculpted muscles weighed a ton. And his sexy eyes had a ring of dark blue surrounding the light part. Was everything about him pretty? And perfect? It was just so annoying.

"Say you're sorry," he growled.

The ten-year-old in her wanted to say "Make me," but there was no doubt he could. "You want me to lie to you?"

"No." His brow furrowed. "Say 'uncle,' then."

Just as she was about to pull his hair, hoping to surprise him enough to find escape, Jo cleared her throat. "Do you need to be rescued Shelby, or are you two going to need a room?"

Did she need rescue? It was kind of nice snuggling up against Nick's hard muscles.

No. He was just being a bully. "Help, please?"

Jo snorted. "I'll go get the bat."

"I'd have gone for the room." Nick moved his mouth next to her ear, his warm breath sending heat racing to her nether regions. "According to your rules, now that I've seen your legs we can sleep together. I'd like that."

Her stomach clenched. He'd probably look pretty darn good naked.

But she wanted Greg. Besides, Nick had to be teasing. He'd never want to have sex with her, especially now that he'd seen her legs. "Liar. According to your survey I'm not your type."

"That used to be my type. Until I met *you*."

Her heart skipped a beat.

Before she could come up with a good retort, Jo returned with her weapon. "I'm counting to three . . ."

Matching Mr. Right

Nick hopped up and held his hand out for Shelby's. She slapped it aside and stood on her own. "I'm not falling for that one."

Turning to her roommate, who stood as if she were ready to hit one out of the park while glowering at Nick, Shelby said, "Thank you, Jo. I appreciate it."

Jo tossed the bat onto the couch and then rolled her eyes. As she headed for the kitchen she said, "My parents are coming over in a few so I'm making breakfast burritos. Is *he* staying?"

Nick beamed a bright smile. "I'd love to. Thanks!"

Jo laughed. "Where do you find them, Shelby?"

When Jo retreated back to the kitchen, Shelby led Nick to the couch and motioned for him to have a seat. She moved the bat aside and drew a deep breath to steady herself after Nick's tempting proposition. "Now, start from the beginning. And why is it your job to find Beth a soul mate, Mr. Fix It?"

When Nick winced, she figured this was going to be good. Or very bad.

✒

Nick berated himself while driving to his mother's house. What had he been thinking? He'd asked Shelby to sleep with him? She was the marriage, two kids, and a dog type if he'd ever seen one. Besides, she'd hate him if she found out what he was up to.

But after feeling all her curves beneath him earlier, there was no doubt the sleeping together part would be incredible, but after that, one of them was bound to kill the other.

Nick chuckled as he recalled how she'd pushed him over. She couldn't weigh more than a hundred and twenty pounds soaking wet, and yet she'd gotten the better of him.

He ran a hand down his face. That shouldn't make her even sexier to him, it should make him very afraid of her. No wonder she wrote about a bad little monkey, because that monkey named Chester should be named Shelby!

But hadn't he told Emily just the other day how much he liked that monkey?

Nope. Shelby had a boyfriend, or a prince, or something. And its name was Greg. Thank God Shelby hadn't agreed to sleep with him. He needed to be sure the opportunity never arose in the future. Mostly because he wasn't sure he could say no if she actually wanted him. He wasn't the house-in-the-'burbs and soccer dad she wanted.

As he pulled into his mother's drive, he came to an abrupt stop. What was his mom doing up on a ladder cleaning out the gutters?

He leapt from the car, slapping his door shut behind him. "Get down from there right now. You're too old to be on a ladder!"

"Too old?" His mom's right brow popped up. Before he'd realized his mistake, a handful of wet, slimy leaves plopped down on top of him.

"Nice, Mom." He wiped slime from his forehead. "That's a move Emily would be proud of."

"You're right. Be sure to tell her." His mother stuck her gloved hand back into the gutter and scooped out more goop.

The "old" remark had been a mistake, and admittedly, his mom was still a beautiful woman, but she *was* fifty-seven.

He blew out a long breath, searching for patience. "Come down and I'll finish that for you."

His mother chuckled as she climbed down the ladder. "Your timing, as always, is impeccable. That was the last of it." When her foot hit the ground, she kissed his cheek. "But I'm entirely too old to put the ladder away, so you can do it. Are you hungry?"

He folded the ladder and hoisted it on his shoulder. "I just had breakfast at Shelby's."

"Ah." His mother smiled knowingly as she removed her gloves.

Nick hung the ladder in the garage and then followed her inside the house. "What does 'ah' mean? And why don't you hire someone to do the gutters? Or call me and I'll do them."

He took his usual place at the old kitchen table, the same sturdy wooden one that had been there his whole life.

"Oh, you'll do it, huh? You mean you'd actually squeeze me into your twenty-four seven work schedule?"

He crossed his arms and stayed silent, refusing to get into that familiar argument.

His mom sighed as she opened the fridge and pulled out a pitcher of tea. "Never mind. I'm perfectly capable. Who do you think has been doing the gutters around here for the past twenty years? And I said 'ah' about Shelby because your father called this morning and told me what happened last night. I hope you were at Shelby's house this morning apologizing?"

Lori came into the kitchen with an empty glass in her hand. "Nick apologized for something? This ought to be good." She plopped down across the table from him.

They were doing it again, outflanking and outnumbering him. "It seems all I'm doing lately is apologizing to women. It's getting old."

"Women? As in plural?" Lori grinned. "Beth wanted you back, didn't she? And you felt all bad, but not bad enough to knock down that big wall around your heart and give love a chance. Although I saw something in the way you looked at Shelby the other night at the book signing."

His mom nodded. "Yes! I saw that too, at the hospital." She turned to Lori, "Maybe Shelby will be the one. Emily would certainly approve of that."

"Stop!" He held up his hands. "Sorry to burst your love bubbles ladies, but Shelby has her sights on some other guy. She and I are just friends." Sort of. She probably wouldn't say so, but he liked *her*.

"Well, friends is a fine place to start." His mom patted his cheek. "Even your dad said you made a good-looking couple. That's why he bid on your date last night."

"No, he bid on Shelby because he's a controlling bastard."

His mom sat down. "Everyone else in the family has forgiven your father but you, Nick. He was trying to be nice last night. He thought Shelby was a lovely woman."

He couldn't sit any longer and stood to pace. "Why do you always give him the benefit of the doubt? He just did that so he could look like the perfect father in front of all those potential clients."

Lori laughed. "The country club set doesn't give a damn about being thought of as good parents. They're more interested in sealing that next deal and who makes the most money among them. Be careful Nick, or you'll become just like them the way you work night and day for the almighty dollar."

Recalling how Shelby's aunt treated her, and her uncle's obsession that she marry just the right guy, weighed heavy on the side of Lori's theory. Not the part about his working and making money, but about the good parent image. "Just because I work hard and make a good living does not make me one of them. I'll never be like dad."

His mom sighed. "You aren't anything like you father, Nick. You're a better person than he could ever be. He knows that, and he's very proud of you. Why do you think your father has never remarried in the past twenty years? He figured out he's not cut out to be a good husband, but that doesn't make him a bad person, just a poor spouse. All he wants now is to be a part of his family's lives. Including yours."

Nick shook his head. "He gave up that right when he asked me to lie to you, Mom. I have to go." He started for the door, but then remembered why he was there. "Lori, do you think Em would want to go to the Broncos game with me and Shelby tomorrow night?"

Lori smiled. "Emily will be beside herself. I think she might be as much in love with Shelby as you are."

"I'm not—"

His sister laughed and turned to their mother. "I told you. The man is completely dense when it comes to feelings. He never saw it with Beth, and now he can't even recognize it in himself."

"Don't play your silly matchmaker games with me. I'm immune. I'll pick Emily up in the limo here at five." He slammed the door behind him to cut off any further ridiculous discussion.

It was futile to argue with them. Either of them. He wished his sister Rachel lived in town. She tended to side with him and helped even out the numbers. Except when the arguments were about his father. Nick was an island there. And he planned to remain one. Let the rest of them pretend their father wasn't so bad. He knew the truth.

Strapping in, he started his car and backed out of the driveway. A week ago his life had been orderly and under control. Since the day he'd met Shelby everything had been out of sync.

But, admittedly, it'd been a nice change.

Maybe he had been working too much.

7

"Chester really liked football. And Julie."
Chester's First Crush

Nick didn't have time to get out of the limo before Shelby emerged from her house for the game on Monday evening. She'd dressed head to toe in Bronco's gear, complete with an oversized jersey, well-worn jeans, orange tennis shoes with blue laces, and her blonde hair had slim streaks of the team colors. There was even a Bronco's logo tattooed on her cheek. Did she go over the top like that because of what he'd told her about other women pretending to like football? Was this her way of saying "in your face?"

Shelby greeted Sam, her uncle's elderly driver, as she slid inside the limo and then sent Emily one of her cute smiles. "Hi, Emily."

"Hi, Shelby!" Emily hopped up and down on her seat. "Is that a real tattoo on your face? And isn't this the biggest car you've ever been in?"

Shelby laughed. "This is my uncle's little limo. You should see the other one. And no, this isn't a real tattoo. It washes off." Shelby finally glanced at him. "Hi. Okay if Emily has one?"

"Sure." While Shelby decorated Em's face, he glanced at his Broncos polo shirt—the kind the coaches wear on the sidelines—feeling underdressed.

After Sam dropped them right in front of the stadium entrance, Shelby led the way, her perfect butt swaying enticingly, to the executive suites. The electric excitement of the fans rushed through him at the prospect of seeing the Broncos attempt to keep their winning streak alive. And who knew? Maybe he'd start a winning streak of his own with Shelby, and she'd finally forgive him for abandoning her at the auction.

Emily's eyes lit with longing as they passed the food vendors. "Look, Uncle Nick, your favorites. Hot dogs, peanuts, and ice cream. Wait, Dots! They're *my* favorite."

When he reached for his wallet, Shelby said, "Don't you dare, Nick. Emily needs to eat dinner first, then Dots."

He pulled a face for Emily's sake. "Shelby's boring, like your mom. Next time, it'll just be you and me, and we'll eat Dots for dinner."

Emily shook her head and slipped her hand into Shelby's. "No. Shelby too."

Shelby met his gaze and beamed a take-that smirk. How could she look so damned sexy dressed like a ten-year-old boy? It made no sense.

"Let's go see what kind of boring food they have waiting for us upstairs, Em." She scooped Emily up in her arms. "Then we'll get you some Dots for dessert. Maybe if your uncle can behave, we'll let him have some too."

Following behind Shelby's cute little ass up the stairs to her uncle's box wasn't going to make behaving any easier.

Her uncle's suite was huge. As Nick held the door open for them, he slipped his hand around Shelby's arm to stop her and whispered, "Is that the mayor and his wife over there?" Shelby hung out with an interesting crowd.

She smiled. "Yes. And standing by the bar are a few former players you may recognize."

Jake Ramsey, the newly retired Probowl hall of famer, in the flesh, called out, "Shelby! You're late, little one. Get over here and catch up before these thugs drink all your uncle's beer!"

Shelby laughed as she accepted their bear hugs and then she introduced them all. The sheer size of the men had Emily's eyes popping.

Nick shook their hands, trying not to look like a little kid meeting Santa for the first time. "Pleasure to meet you guys."

And when he spotted the "boring grub," he stopped dead in his tracks. "I expected hot dogs and burgers. Nothing like this." His mouth watered as he eyed the Kobe steak, crab cakes, pasta, and huge baked potatoes with all the fixings. And of course, the obligatory brats, hotdogs, and hamburgers.

Shelby handed him a china plate. "Welcome to Uncle Jack's world. Hurry and load up, the game starts in a half hour." Then she caught one of the passing waiters and asked him to bring three cups of Dots for dessert.

෴

Shelby stole a quick glance at Nick. His plate was empty. Again. He'd gone back three times for more. Seems he was having a good time filling that perfect six-pack-abs belly.

She'd never forget the look on his face when he'd seen her get into the limo. It was awesome, but the suspicious glances he'd been sending her way told her he still didn't think she was a real fan.

Whatever. Better to keep him guessing. More fun that way.

It was almost kick-off so they moved to the front seats to watch the game while they ate dessert. She called her friend Michael, the mayor's son, over. "Look what we've got, Mikey. Dots!" She handed her cup to him, saving room for some nachos later.

"Thanks, Shelby. Love you!" Michael had Down syndrome and was the sweetest man she'd ever met. He dug in as he went back to sit with his parents.

After the game had started, she and Nick were captivated, but Emily didn't seem to be as interested. Shelby leaned close to Emily and whispered, "Mikey gets bored during the game sometimes, so he always brings a bag of toys. I'm sure he'd share with you."

Emily frowned. "But he's a grown-up. He's probably got boring toys."

"Mikey's a special grown-up. While his body gets older, he still likes the same things kids do. He's a really sweet man."

Emily ate a few bites of her treat as she considered. "Sort of like Peter Pan, but real?"

"Sort of." She gave Emily a hug. Em was an adorable kid who made Shelby want a little Emily of her own. "You should go play with him when you're done."

Em nodded while stuffing Dots in her mouth. "'Kay."

Nick sat on the edge of his seat, a beer in his hand, with a mile-wide grin. She'd been careful to keep her distance, not looking for a repeat of what happened on her living room floor. She was focusing on Greg, who'd be home in a few days. But Nick's joy was contagious. "Having a good time?"

"Nah. It's been almost as bad as that charity thing the other night." He leaned back and slipped an arm around her shoulder, pulling her close. Then he moved his mouth to her ear and whispered, "You look even hotter in that jersey than you did in the red dress."

Her stomach did that clenching thing again. "Personally, I'm going with the tux on you. That's some lame excuse for fan wear you're rocking."

"You'd put any fan to shame with your gear." As he watched the game, he slid his wrist to the back of her padded seat, and his fingers gently massaged her neck.

She barely resisted the urge to purr.

As the quarterback let loose of the ball, Nick's hand stilled. After the play was over, his fingers moved in small circles again. "I can't believe you know so many ex-players. And you're on a first name basis with the mayor and his family? How do I get myself invited for the next home game?"

She should lean away from his soft touch, but it was hypnotic. She'd missed the simple pleasure of a gentle caress. But he was probably just doing that to suck up to her and get invited back. "Have I mentioned how much I like nachos with my beer?"

He grinned as he plucked her empty beer cup from her hand. "How about I start by getting you a refill?"

"Good plan." When he left, she turned her attention back to the game. What was she doing? Letting him touch her like that? She didn't even like him. Well, that wasn't entirely true, she didn't *dis*like him. He just bugged the heck out of her sometimes. Most of the time. But then there were those rare moments . . . no. It was just hormones. Or pheromones? She'd have to look that up. Nick was the best-looking man she'd ever known and it clouded her thinking. She should go join her buddies and forget about him.

Em was happy playing with Mikey so she crossed the suite to talk to her gigantic pals.

Jake slipped his big arm around her waist and pulled her against his side. "Shelby darling. When you gonna break down and marry me?"

"I can't take a man serious who asks without a rock." She slid her arm around his waist and returned his hug. "Besides, I'm afraid of your wife. She's a lot bigger than me."

He chuckled. "Everyone's a lot bigger than you. Ooh, did you see that?" He pointed down field and they lost themselves in the game. A few minutes later, Nick appeared by her side with a beer and a plate of nachos. She unwrapped herself from Jake's big arm and accepted them. "Thanks."

Jake lifted his chin in Nick's direction. "Yo. Be good to her man, or you got me and my men here to answer to."

Nick's chest puffed out as he crossed his arms. "Seems to me, it's you who better watch out. You just had your arm around my date. Want to step outside?"

When Jake's eyes narrowed, Shelby's stomach took a dive. What the heck was Nick doing? The man outweighed him by at least a hundred and fifty pounds. "Jake, Nick was just—"

Then Jake's face lit with a big grin. "Well, now. That took some big cojones, didn't it?" He slapped Nick on the back so hard he took a step forward. "I think you'll do just fine for our little Shelby. Step up on over here and let me buy you a drink . . . or three."

Nick sent her a smug grin as he disappeared into the big cloud of testosterone surrounding the bar.

Men.

She shook her head and went to check on Emily.

Emily and Mikey were working on an impressive castle made with Legos. "Hey guys." She stuck her plate of nachos out, but got silent head shakes in return. Evidently building stuff with Legos was serious business. She'd never had Legos as a kid. It was halftime, so maybe she'd give it a try.

Between gooey, cheesy bites of nachos, and swigs of beer to wash it down, she went to work.

Just as she was putting the pièce de la résistance on the top, Nick's hands spread across her shoulders and gave them a gentle squeeze. "That might be the most pathetic attempt at a house I've ever seen."

"That's because it's not a house. It's a castle."

He laughed. "Then it's even worse. Best to stick to using the good side of your brain writing books and finding soul mates."

"I don't recall seeing Lego Building Inspector on your application, buddy. And the other side of my brain works just fine." She swatted his hands off her shoulders for good measure. And because she was liking his touch just a little too much.

Nick called out, "Em and Mike? We need a ruling over here. Shelby's kinda bad at this, right?"

Mikey said, "Yeah. But she's nice."

Em scrunched up her nose. "She did her best, Uncle Nick."

Ouch.

Shelby reexamined her masterpiece with a serious critic's eye and . . . had to agree. It pretty much sucked.

Nick's blue eyes shone with victory so she said, "Rule number three in the dating manual states: always compliment your date, even if she creates crooked Lego castles. Clearly you need to do your dating homework, Caldwell."

"My bad." Nick smiled so sweetly it made her heart do a funny little jig. He held out a hand to help her off the floor, so she let him.

"Forward that manual to my e-mail and I'll do my best to make you proud. But halftime is almost over. Want to go watch the rest of the game with the guys?"

With the guys? Did he mean *her* guys? "You come to one game and you think you're automatically in the club? It doesn't work that way. We've all been tight for years. You have to earn your membership."

"They said any guy you're with has to be all right. So, I'm in. Jake invited me back next week. He said he'd leave my name at the gate. How cool is that?"

She rolled her eyes. "Standardless Neanderthals, each and every one of you."

"Is standardless even a word?"

"You dare to doubt a writer? Maybe you'd like to put your money where your mouth is?"

"Never mind. But I'm going to google that later just to keep you honest." Nick wrapped his arm around her waist and tugged her toward the bar. "This is the best date I've ever had, Shelby."

"That's not saying much. You don't do real dating. Remember?"

His lips tilted in an I'm-a-little-bit-drunk way. "That's going to have to change now."

"Yeah, well to get to this level of date, you're going to have to learn how to get past the first meet. Are you willing to fit me into your ridiculous work schedule so I can help you do that?"

"Absolutely."

Shelby leaned closer, peering into his eyes. Was it just the beer talking? "So instead of me finding you another sex partner, you're really going to give dating an honest chance?"

He pondered for a moment. Then he nodded sharply. "If dating can be like today, then I'm in! Let's go, the game just started."

※

Nick slid next to Shelby in the limo after they dropped Em off. Their next stop would be Shelby's house.

Her pretty blonde hair fell over her shoulder as she texted on her phone, arranging a lunch date for him the next day. It'd be hard to top the evening they'd just had. He was still enjoying a happy buzz from trying to keep up with those ex-players who could really pack the beers away. But the best part was figuring out that Shelby was a true football fan. The way she'd gotten in Jake's face and argued a call with him had been . . . impressive!

He needed to kiss her.

If the kiss was no good, then they'd just be friends. That'd be fine too, because Shelby was the first woman he'd ever wanted to be friends with. But mostly, he just liked being with her.

When the limo stopped, Shelby leaned through the window and had a quiet conversation with Sam before she opened her door. "'Nite, Nick. Bring Beth by the café around ten thirty, okay? Your lunch date tomorrow is with a woman named Lisa. We're meeting at eleven thirty at a restaurant near her office. You're driving us."

"Got it." He leaned forward and told Sam he'd be right back and then followed her. "Wait up, Shelby. A guy's supposed to walk his date to her front door." He caught up with her and wrapped his arm around her waist. "And then I should probably kiss you good night. It still works that way, right?"

Shelby frowned as she dug through her purse for her keys. "You're on a football and alcohol high, Nick. In the morning light, you'd never want to kiss *me*."

"Untrue. You are the most interesting and sexy woman I've ever met." He brushed his lips against her cheek. "I've wanted to kiss you since the first time we met."

"You're drunk, pal. It's impairing your memory." Shelby shook her head and continued her search for the keys.

"Just a little and I'll prove it. The first time we met, you wore a soft cream-colored top that gave just a peek at the goods, and dark pants that made your ass look fantastic." He leaned closer and nibbled on her ear. "What are you afraid of, Shelby?"

He knew she was way too competitive a person not to take that bait.

"Afraid? I'm not—wait." Shelby stopped her search for her keys. "You remember what I was wearing?" Shelby stared into his eyes, frowning, and hopefully considering. "Oh, all right Mr. Beer Goggles, give it your best shot!"

Thank God for her competitive streak. That'd probably make her fun in bed too.

He drew in a deep breath, grabbed her amazing ass with both hands, and pulled her against him. Then he leaned down and laid his lips on her full, soft ones.

Better than he'd imagined. Perfect fit.

When her lips parted, inviting him to take more, he did just that. His tongue caressed hers as his hand slid up her side and landed on her soft breast. When he gave a gentle squeeze, she moaned, dropped her purse, and threw her hands around his neck.

Shelby's fingers sliding through his hair sent hot waves of desire racing through his veins, heating his blood. His mind floated somewhere it'd never gone before, somewhere warm and inviting and outside of his body.

But then she abruptly ended the kiss and pulled away.

She sucked in a deep breath and then licked her perfect lips, making him want to dive back in for more. As he started forward, she held a hand to his chest.

"Wait. Stop." She blinked as if confused. "Okay. You're pretty good at that, but I'm interested in Greg. A guy who wants what I want. A family and kids. So I can't do this, Nick."

Talk of husbands and kids was like a bucket of cold water crashing over his head, squelching his desires. Besides, he was a lying bastard and didn't deserve her. He kept forgetting that part when he was around her.

"No, you're right." He backed up a step to regain his composure. No woman had ever made him feel like that with a simple kiss before. It couldn't be good. She'd have him wrapped around her finger in no time. "I had a good time tonight. Thanks."

He turned and started to leave but couldn't do it. He needed something more. Turning back around, he wrapped her up in his arms and lifted her against his chest for a hard hug. Then he laid a soft kiss on her forehead. "A really good time. Thank you." With a pat on her fine ass, he dropped her to her feet and said, "'Nite, Summer Sinclair."

8

> "Sometimes what Chester wants isn't always what's best for him."
> ***Chester's Tough Choice***

Shelby tucked the covers under her chin and smiled as she stared at the thin lines of sunshine streaking across her bedroom's ceiling. Nick had called her by her real name last night. It shouldn't have touched her so deeply but it had. Because in her heart, that's who she was. Summer Sinclair, not Shelby Marx. If she tried hard enough she could still conjure the sound of her mother's voice sweetly calling her name.

And then to make things even more confusing, Nick had remembered what she'd worn the first time they'd met. She'd never known a guy who'd paid attention like that.

No other man had ever kissed her like that either. Boy, could Nick kiss! Her lips warmed at the memory.

Wondering what a good time Nick would be in bed wasn't helping her stay on track.

She needed to forget about Nick and concentrate on a more obtainable goal, like Greg.

Greg knew about her legs, although he'd never seen them. As a doctor, Greg would be used to seeing scars like hers. He'd take them in stride, like Nick had.

Her heart warmed as she recalled how Nick had made her feel whole again, instead of like damaged goods, after he'd seen her ugly legs. But Nick was off-limits. He'd said he'd never marry and have kids. She needed to take him at his word. Just ignore the way the man made her brain go stupid when he kissed her.

Back to Greg.

When she saw Greg at his party tomorrow, she'd invite him to the football game on Sunday. That'd be a good date. He'd been out of the country for two years, so he'd probably enjoy seeing a live game. And it wouldn't seem like she was actually asking him on a date, more like inviting him to an event because she had extra seats. Yup. That'd be perfect. She didn't want to scare him off by seeming too pushy. But she needed to push harder to get him to see her as a woman, or she'd never get past first base. How much was too much?

Shelby smashed her spare pillow over her face and screamed into it. Why did men, dating, and kissing have to be so complicated? Although that was probably a good thing because it kept her Cyrano business running.

Thinking of work, she needed to get up and go to the café. She wanted to get some things done before she met with Nick and Beth later.

Would it be awkward seeing Nick again? No. He'd probably already forgotten all about their kiss. Throwing the covers back she slid out of bed and headed to the bathroom to get ready.

Matching Mr. Right

After she was all ready to roll, she grabbed a to-go cup of coffee and headed out. When Shelby crossed the café's threshold at 8:30 a.m., Jo threw a starched apron her way. "Charlie, Susan, and Sheila all called in sick. I've got help on the way, but it'll be a bit. Take the register, please."

Shelby tied the apron around her waist and dove in. There must've been thirty people in line. Hopefully they'd all want plain coffee or something easy. She hadn't run the front counter in a long time.

After a few hours, the line was under control and the proper way to make a mucho-mocha latte had surfaced from the depths of her brain. And thankfully, two of the replacement workers had arrived. One more person and she'd be able to call it quits. How did Jo do it every day?

She slipped a hunk of stray hair behind her ear, then turned to help the next person in line. When she glanced up she spotted Nick a few people away, looking all tall, tantalizing . . . and tasty. Her lips tingled at the memory of their kiss.

Then a slender, gorgeous blonde whispered something in his ear, sending an arrow of reality straight through Shelby's heart.

Beth.

She was a freaking goddess. The woman should be required to hand out sunglasses to shield the unknowing victim's eyes from the beauty that radiated from her glowing, perfect skin. She wore a tailored navy suit jacket with a short skirt that highlighted her mile-long, unblemished legs, and a silky blouse that left no question that God had been good to her in the breast department. And her shoes? They were to die for. Tall, strappy, and sexy.

Compared to that, Shelby probably looked like the last day-old donut left under the glass dome in a greasy-spoon diner.

Thankfully, Shelby's replacement arrived, putting an end to her pity party, so she gladly handed over her apron, "Thanks, Gina. Have a good day."

When she leaned down to retrieve her purse, a pair of male arms wrapped around her from behind, pinning her hands to her side, and then he lifted her off of her feet.

She called out, "Hey!" *What the heck?*

Shelby saw Nick push Beth aside before he started toward the register.

When the mystery man's warm breath heated her ear, repulsion skittered up her spine. Then he kissed her cheek and whispered, "It's been way too long. How are you, honey?"

At the sound of the familiar voice, Shelby's thumping heart settled a little.

It was Greg!

"Hi. You scared me."

"Sorry. Couldn't resist."

When he dropped her to her feet, she spun around and gave him a hard hug.

After a few moments, she reluctantly let go and took a step back, drawing in the sight of him. Greg, like Nick, was tall, but Greg was blond and blue-eyed dreamy.

Suddenly her brain cleared enough to realize he'd called her honey. Babe would have been better, but now was not the time to analyze his every word. She'd do that later.

While she was having a private party in her head, Nick's hand slipped around her waist, plastering her against his side. "What's going on, Shelby?"

She lifted her chin and stared into Nick's narrowed eyes. She'd probably startled him when she'd panicked for a moment, there. But he'd seemed genuinely worried about her, and that was kind of nice.

"This is Greg. I should've known it was just him. He was always sneaking up on me like that when we were kids. But I didn't think I'd see him until tomorrow."

Greg beamed a bright smile. "I got in a day early and I couldn't wait to see what you and Jo have done with the place. It's fantastic, Shelby." Greg held out a hand to Nick. "Greg Westin."

Nick slowly removed his hand from her waist and clasped Greg's hand. "Nick." Then he turned to her. "So, is your little reunion over? We have a meeting, right?"

Ignoring Nick's snippy tone, she replied. "I'll be right with you." Then she smiled at Greg. "The café is Jo's baby, I just help out sometimes. I'm super proud of her."

"Me too. Where is she?"

"Right through there." She pointed toward the swinging doors.

"Thanks. Really great to see you, Shelby." He waved and headed to the kitchen.

And then it hit her. She must look awful! She was sweaty, and her hair had probably gone limp from being around all the steam. Maybe she could repair the damage before he came back.

She grabbed her purse and laptop from under the counter, but before she could slip away to freshen up, Nick's long fingers wrapped around her upper arm and stopped her.

Slapping a twenty on the counter with his other hand, Nick said, "We need two coffees, black, and whatever you're having, barista! Since when do you work here?"

Was he mad at her? "I own part of this, so when half the staff calls in with the flu, I help out. It's a particularly nasty bug this year so if you haven't already, you should get a flu shot. I'm thankful I did."

"I never get sick." Nick leaned closer and scowled. "So, that was Greg-the-surfer-dude-prince, huh? Does he often scare the crap out of you?"

What had crawled up Nick's butt? Maybe he was mad that all the alcohol he'd consumed the night before had led to his kissing someone like her when he was used to flawless Beth.

"Greg was just happy to see me, so what?" Shelby laid her things down, poured the drinks and tucked them into a cardboard carrier.

After slipping his twenty into the tray, she shoved it into his gut.

Hard.

He grunted, but then motioned for her to go first.

After giving her tarnished knight-in-shining-armor an eye roll, she headed toward the dining area.

Beth joined them, slipping her arm through Nick's bent one, and pulled him close. "I have an eleven o'clock so could we move this along? That is, if your spat is over?"

Nick slapped the coffee carrier onto the table. Then he drew a deep breath and composed himself. "Shelby Marx, Beth Gunderson."

Beth nodded and then slowly slithered her long body onto a chair. Man that was a sexy move. Maybe Shelby'd have to give that a try sometime when she went to dinner with Greg. But it probably didn't look nearly as sexy since she was five-two instead of five-ten.

Nick cleared his throat. He stood behind her, holding her chair and frowning.

Since when did Nick pull out chairs for her? "Thank you?"

As she sat down, she decided not to think about how her makeup had probably sweated off and her mascara streaked.

It'd be futile. "Beth, thanks for coming today. I see you filled out the questionnaire online last night, so I just need to—"

"Just find me someone like Nick, and we're good." Beth laid her hand on Nick's forearm and gazed deeply into his eyes.

Shelby couldn't pinpoint why that bugged the hell out of her, but it did. "Okay. But are you looking to date this person or are you looking for something like you and Nick had?"

Beth sighed. "Dating is fine, but I usually know if a man's right within a few moments, so doing coffee dates or a quick lunch is all I want at this point." She looked at her cell phone then stood. "Why don't you find me some candidates? I'll free my lunch hour all of next week. Do the same for Nick. He needs to see what's out there. Sometimes the grass looks a whole lot greener until you have to date it!" Beth sent Nick an eyebrow hitch and then stalked away.

Shelby laughed. "Someone isn't happy about giving up her sex partner. So where should we set up your lunch dates next week? Oh, I know. We could do them at the park . . . on the grass."

"Funny." Nick scowled as he plucked the twenty-dollar bill from the holder and slid it in front of her.

"I was just kidding."

When his jaw clenched and he refused to look her in the eye, remorse sat like a lead ball in her belly.

Okay, clearly he was growing on her. She probably even cared for him a little. But he was still the most annoying man she'd ever met. And the sexiest, but that part she needed to put aside.

She slipped Nick's twenty to the new busboy as he walked by, and then laid her hand over his big warm one and gave it a squeeze. "What's wrong, Nick?"

He shook his head. "Nothing." Then he lifted his head and stared into her eyes as if searching for something.

Confused by the emotion in his gaze, she said, "Are you mad about our kiss—"

"Sorry to interrupt." Greg slipped into an empty chair across from her. "But Jo said you wouldn't mind, Shelby."

She glanced at Nick's tightly entwined fingers around hers. How that had that happened she wasn't sure, but it felt nice. Maybe he wasn't as mad at her as she thought.

But then Greg's presence reminded her to keep her eye on the ball, so she started to untangle their fingers. When she tried to slip her hand away, Nick tightened his grip.

Dammit. She couldn't wrestle her hand away without looking like an idiot, but what would Greg think? She'd make Nick pay for that later.

Greg beamed a bright smile at her. "I have to go. I'm going to surprise Dad at his office. But I wanted to tell you that some of the guys from the neighborhood are going to be at the party. We'd hoped we could talk you into playing receiver. The five of us went undefeated that one summer, remember?"

Her stomach took a dive. "I don't think I'll be dressed for that . . ."

"Just bring some sweats to change into. We're all looking forward to it. We've all missed you, Shelby." Greg stood and pushed his chair back under the table.

"Umm. Okay. See you tomorrow." All the gang missed her, or had *he* missed her?

Greg lifted a hand in Nick's direction. "Nice to meet you." Then he turned to her, "Bye, Shelby."

She sent him a finger wave with her free hand and then took a sip from her cup as she pondered the situation. One step forward, two steps back. Should she play or not? She wouldn't want to disappoint him.

After Greg left, Nick slowly slid his hand from hers, then crossed his arms. "So your prince, who you haven't seen for two years, who your gooey heart longs for, just wants to play football with you?"

"No! It's just . . . none of your damned business." He'd hit way too close to the truth, and that holding-her-hand-hostage thing hadn't been funny. She packed up her laptop and stood to leave. "Did you read the stuff I forwarded you about first dates last night?"

"Yup." His grin quickly faded as he stood and walked out beside her. He beat her to the exit and yanked the glass door open. "I'm parked just over there."

She was parked right in front and really didn't want to talk to him at the moment, so she pressed her fob and unlocked her car door. "I'll just meet you there."

"I can't believe you drive a Prius." He tilted his head as he circled her car. "Pop the hood. I want to see how many mice are under there."

"You know what, Nick? It's going to be tough finding you a woman as hilarious as you!" She slid behind the wheel and slammed the door. She'd had enough of his smart comments.

His knuckle tapped on her window.

She rolled it down. "What?"

Leaning inside, he shot her a big grin. "Is my lunch date a brunette? You said they were better in—"

"Yes. Now go away." She splayed her fingers across his face, pushed his big head out, then rolled up her window. He'd get a brunette the next time too, all right. And she had just the one in mind. His name was Jordan. A good friend with a wicked sense of humor who was almost as pretty as Nick. Too bad for all the women in the world, Jordan preferred men. Teach Nick to sabotage her quest for Greg by holding her hand like that.

He knocked again.

She lowered her window a scant inch and raised a brow.

"We should think green and ride together. But I'm not cramming myself into that Prius. I'll drive." He opened her door, reached in, and wrapped his large hand around her arm. She grabbed her things just as her body took flight.

His firm grasp propelled her across the rough pavement, tugging her toward his sexy car.

"Maybe I don't want to be trapped in a car with an obnoxious man like you." She lifted her key remote over her shoulder, beeping her car locked.

"I love when you're feisty and pissed off. I'll bet you'd be fun under the sheets that way too."

"My sheets are reserved for Greg. And we need to discuss your bad attitude toward him! What do you think Greg thought when you held on to my hand like that?"

Nick's jaw clenched as he opened her door. "He doesn't deserve you, Shelby."

"And you'd know this, how?" After he'd rounded to his side and joined her, she buckled her seat belt and glared at him.

He blew out a breath before he zipped into traffic. "You need a guy who wants to make love to you, not play football with you. What does he have that I don't?"

She snorted. "The desire for a wife and kids, for starters."

He shifted gears and floored it through a yellow light. "Why can't you just sleep with a guy and have fun? No strings attached."

She'd wondered that about herself too. Often. "I guess because then I wouldn't be me?"

He opened his mouth to respond, then snapped it shut. "Good point. But then the guy you pick is too blind to see what a beautiful woman you are?" He turned and briefly stared into her eyes. "You deserve better, Shelby."

She started to defend Greg, but Nick raised a hand to cut her off. "It's how I see it. And I'm done fighting about Gary!"

She poked him in the arm. "Until you admit holding my hand hostage in front of *Greg* shows what a jerk you are, we're not even close to being done!"

"Okay, I'm a jerk. But at least I'd know what to do with the sexiest woman to ever cross my path." The lust in his gaze threatened to make her traitorous girl parts combust.

She crossed her arms and closed her eyes, blocking out his alluring baby-blue ones. "You're impossible."

When he chuckled, she winced.

Good come back, Shelby. That'd rate about a Three from the East German judge.

Her anger slowly dissipated as she leaned back and enjoyed the fast ride. She really missed her Porsche.

Nick's comment about why she couldn't just have a fun fling bounced around her brain.

Who was he to talk? She turned to him and asked, "Have you ever been in love, Nick?"

He shook his head. "Nope."

"If you've never been in love, you can't know what you're missing. Dating will be good for you. You work too much. You need to find someone you can have fun with and who'll show you how nice a real relationship can be."

"I had fun with you last night. Dump the prince and I'll show you what it's like to have great sex with a real man."

"No thank you, Mr. Shallow." She huffed out a breath.

Would she consider it if she thought Nick would take her seriously? But he wouldn't. He'd sleep with her a few times and then move on when he became bored. But the sex would probably be amazing.

When they arrived at her favorite cozy Italian restaurant, Nick held the door open for her. She couldn't argue with Nick's manners. It was about the only thing she couldn't argue with him about.

The little tables covered with red-and-white checked table cloths all had wine bottles with colorful wax dripping down the sides at their center. The scent of garlic and warm, freshly made bread made Shelby's stomach beg for a big slice of their to-die-for lasagna.

The owner, Michael, waved from the kitchen. "We got you all set up like last time, Shelby. You want the usual?"

"Yes, please!" She loved supporting small mom-and-pop restaurants like hers and Jo's. Although, Jo had bigger plans for theirs one day.

She wrapped her hand around Nick's big arm and tugged him to the rear, weaving through the tables full of diners. "Okay, so you'll sit here with your back to the wall and wait for Lisa. She said she's wearing a blue silk shirt and black slacks. I'll be over there where she can't see me but you'll be able to. Try not to make eye contact with me when I speak in your ear. It's a mistake first-timers often make."

"Got it." Nick accepted the ear piece and popped it in. "So, what does Lisa do for a living?"

"That's an excellent question you should ask *her*, not me. Have a seat and I'll go to my table and we'll do a quick sound check."

Nick nodded and pulled his chair out.

Shelby took her place, grabbed a menu so she could hide her face when Lisa walked by, and then said softly, "Can you hear me, Nick?"

"Roger that."

"Good. Hey, put your phone away."

He frowned at the screen. "Why? She's not here yet."

"Don't make me come over there. Put it away, now!"

"I just want to answer this one—"

"Nick. Stop. You don't want to miss that magical moment. The one where she's searching for you, you're looking for her, and when your eyes finally meet, you both realize at the same time you've found the one you're looking for."

He laughed as he tucked his phone away. "You should be writing chick flicks instead of children's books, Shelby. That's the most ridiculous—" He glanced up. "She just walked in. And yet, there's not even an ounce of that magical mojo crap you just described. I'm feeling totally ripped off here—"

"Shhhh! She's going to think you're talking to yourself like a crazy person."

When Lisa reached his table, Nick stood and held his hand out. "Hi. I'm Nick. Are you Lisa?"

"Yes, nice to meet you, Nick. Shelby described you well. I knew it was you instantly." Nick shook the tall, slender, dark-haired beauty's hand and then pulled her chair out for her.

So far, so good. Lisa was a new client so it'd be good to see how she operated too.

When a big plate of lasagna appeared before Shelby, she smiled and thanked her waiter. As she listened in, Lisa did all the talking and Nick gave her short one or two word answers. He hadn't paid any attention at all to his homework. He was breaking all the conversation rules.

She dug into her meal, hopeful that Nick would get a clue and ask Lisa something.

When he seemed more interested in the menu than his date Shelby said, "Thank her for meeting you on her lunch hour, then ask what she does for a living." She'd chosen Lisa because she was a lawyer, like Beth, hoping it'd be easier for Nick to find common ground.

Nick smiled and asked Lisa the question.

Lisa laid her menu down. "Well, I just recently made a huge life change. I quit my job because I felt stifled and unable to embrace my beliefs to the fullest. So, I bought a little shop nearby. We sell crystals and hard-to-get items for those who wish to cast spells and practice voodoo."

Nick blinked. "Spells? And voodoo?"

Shelby stopped eating and strained to hear as Lisa said, "Yes. I omitted that part on my profile because many people are closed-minded about my lifestyle. I can talk to the dead sometimes too."

"The dead too, huh?" Nick's brow furrowed. "And spells. Wow. That's . . . interesting."

Lisa nodded as she perused the menu again. "Yes, I'm quite good at them, actually. You seem a little uptight. If you'd like, I could cook you up a good cleansing spell."

Shelby laughed so hard she nearly spit out her lasagna.

Nick said, "No. I'm good. But thanks. So, what are we going to order?" He lifted his menu in front of his face and whisper-screamed, "Get me out of this. Now, Shelby!"

This was the perfect punishment for what he did to her in front of Greg. No way was she shutting it down. It was entirely too much fun to watch him suffer. "It's good practice. Ask her if she knows any *love* spells."

He growled, "Hell, no!" before he lowered his menu and broke another rule by glaring straight at her.

She answered him with a smug smile as she ate her awesome lasagna. She'd have to remember to update Lisa's profile when she got back home.

Nick tugged at his collar the whole time their waiter took their order. When he glanced her way again, she almost felt sorry for him. But it'd be interesting to see what he did in this kind of situation, so she ignored his pleading eyes and buttered some more warm bread.

"Look, Lisa." Nick ran a hand down his face. "You seem like a great person and all, but I have to be honest here. I'm one of those closed-minded people you mentioned. I don't want to be disingenuous and pretend I think we'd be a good match. So maybe—"

Lisa lifted a hand and cut him off. "Yes, I know. I read you as soon as I touched your hand. I also saw that you're in love with another woman. You should get in touch with and accept those feelings because she'd make you happy." Lisa called the waiter over and canceled her order. Then she said to Nick, "But you need to figure out how to forgive yourself before you'll be truly happy. It was nice to meet you. Be well, Nick."

Because Shelby was still processing Lisa's words, she forgot to hide behind her menu. Lisa winked at her as she passed by.

Shelby picked up her plate and slipped into Lisa's vacated chair as the waiter placed a plate of lasagna in front of Nick. "Okay, that last thing she said is freaking me out. How could she know? About the forgiving yourself thing. Maybe she's legit?"

Nick laughed. "Shelby, think about it. Most people carry guilt about something, it was just a lucky guess." He took a big bite of lasagna. "This is amazing!"

"I know, right? It's my favorite." She took another bite off her own plate and pondered the rest of what Lisa said. "Could the other woman she thought you were in love with be Beth? You were with her for a few years."

Nick's fork stopped mid-bite. He stared into her eyes for a moment before he slowly shook his head. "No. It's not Beth."

"Oh, okay." A weird sense of relief filled her as she finished off her meal.

When she was done, she pushed her empty plate forward and watched Nick eat. Joyous lust for his rich, cheesy lasagna lit his handsome face. He probably had that same expression when he made love to a woman.

After he scooped up the last of the red sauce with his garlic bread, he glanced up and caught her staring. "What?"

"Nothing." She pulled herself together and held out her hand. "I need my Bluetooth back."

He handed it over. "This didn't do *me* any good, but you seemed to enjoy it. Next time, can you hit the mute button when you're laughing your ass off? It's distracting."

"Okay. But when she got to the part about you needing a cleanse . . ." Shelby started laughing all over again.

"Yeah, that was hilarious." Sarcasm laced his tone, but Nick smiled as he signed his name to the bill. "Let's go."

She waved to the owner on the way out. When they got to Nick's car she held her hand out and waggled her fingers. "Keys, please. I want to drive back."

"I *never* let anyone else drive my car." Nick's grin grew wicked as he tugged his keys from his pocket. "But maybe I'd be willing to make an exception." He leaned closer and whispered, "If you kiss me again."

The heat smoldering in his eyes sent a bolt of desire straight to her belly.

She wanted to. But she really, really shouldn't. "Deal."

Nick's brows spiked as he dropped the keys into her hand.

She stood on her toes and kissed his cheek.

"That's not nearly good enough." Nick reached for his keys.

She held them behind her back. "Too bad. Next time you'll just have to be more specific."

Laughing, Shelby hightailed it to the driver's side before Nick changed his mind. She was a good driver and couldn't wait to scare the crap out of him on the way home.

9

"Chester loved his bright-red sneakers. Hopefully, all the girls would too!"
Chester Goes To His First Birthday Party

"Mirror, mirror on the wall, will this be the sexiest outfit of them all?" Shelby chanted into her full-length mirror as she slipped a dangly earring into place. She wore a scoop neck pink top with a push up bra underneath that worked the girls nicely, super tight jeans, high heeled ankle boots and a tight cropped leather jacket to top it all off. Her hair was poofier than usual and she'd given herself dark, smoky eyes. "Or do I look like a hooker?"

Jo laughed. "You look hot! If Greg doesn't notice you in that, then he's either blind or into men now." She tossed Shelby's bag to her. "Come on, we're late. You can drive seeing as I'm nearly out of gas."

Shelby caught her purse and then dug the keys out. "See, that's the beauty of a Prius. I'm rarely out of gas."

Jo waited by the car for Shelby to pop the locks before sliding her long body inside. "You're just still trying to convince yourself you don't miss the Porsche."

"True. I drove Nick's yesterday and it was fantastic!" Probably best not to share the part about how Nick wouldn't let her out until he'd gotten his proper kiss. Although, there was nothing proper about it—it was smokin' hot. And it was the last time she'd let him kiss her, no matter how incredible he was at it.

Shelby laid a hand over her nervous stomach and refocused on the mission at hand. Greg. "Thank goodness for this rain. No touch football for me tonight."

"Yeah. That was a lucky break. Would you have played if it hadn't been raining?"

Shelby had asked herself the same question. It was Nick's cocky voice in her head that had convinced her she wouldn't have played. Just to prove Nick was wrong about Greg. Probably.

"Nope."

When they got to Jo's parents' house, cars lined the sidewalk for two solid blocks. Everyone in Denver must be at the party. Greg had always been a popular guy.

Shelby had no intention of ruining her hair by walking in the wind and rain for a half mile, so she pulled up to her aunt and uncle's house next door and parked under their large portico. "Let's make a dash for it."

Shelby linked arms with Jo, ducked under their umbrella, and made a run for the gate in the wall that separated their properties. Just as they'd both done a thousand times in their haste to tell each other the latest news, or to gossip about boys when they were kids. Thankfully, once they crossed the side yard, the kitchen door was unlocked and they stepped inside.

After they greeted Jo's mom, who was organizing the servers in the kitchen, Jo wandered off to talk to one of their girlfriends while Shelby went on the hunt for Greg. Normally he was easy to spot because he was so tall, but Shelby, being particularly short and in a huge crowd of people, couldn't find him. She needed to move to higher ground.

She climbed the stairs to the catwalk that overlooked the cavernous great room on one side and the dining room that could seat twenty on the other. From above she finally spotted the top of Greg's head leaning close to a woman whose giant breasts threatened to spill out of her flimsy top. She'd recognize those bazookas anywhere, as would half the guys from their high school class. Most had handled them back in the day. They belonged to Shelby's high school nemesis, Tiffany Baker.

Shelby's courage took a hike. She felt like a fourteen-year-old again. How could she compete against Tiffany, a girl who got any guy she set her sights on?

Crossing the catwalk to Jo's old bedroom, Shelby slipped inside and closed the door behind her. She turned on the light, made her way to Jo's bathroom and stared at her reflection in the mirror.

She needed to man up. Her plan was going to work, it had to. Greg was different from most guys. He had a serious and deep side that compelled him to volunteer his time and talent for others. He'd never be swayed by a big set of cha-chas.

She hoped.

After swiping more lip gloss on, she threw her shoulders back and walked out of Jo's old room. She'd waited two years for this moment and she would not fail. Besides, maybe she'd killed enough time so that Tiffany had moved on to her next victim.

From her perch above, Shelby found Greg again. Thankfully, he was talking to the neighborhood guys, so it was time to make her move. She headed for the stairs, and just as her foot hit the bottom rung her aunt called out, "There you are. I've been looking all over for you."

She'd known her aunt and uncle would be at the party, but she'd hoped to say hello and then avoid them for the rest of the evening. "Hi, how are you?" She peered past her aunt's shoulder to find Greg, but he was gone again, dammit. He was a freaking moving target.

"Exhausted after the auction, but recovered now." She took Shelby's arm and motored her in the direction of the dining room. "There's someone here you need to meet. His mother plays tennis with me at the club, and he's an investment banker. His name is James Worthy."

Shelby dug in her heels, halting their forward progress. "Not tonight. I'm supposed to meet someone else here."

Her aunt's gaze burned a hot trail of disapproval from Shelby's head to her shoes. "Dressed like . . . that? You're sending the wrong message with that outfit, Shelby. You're of the age now that you need to start worrying about settling down. And we both know that your pool of men to choose from is limited because of your legs. Men don't seriously date girls dressed like you, they just want to sleep with them."

"Awesome, because that's the plan! I need a drink, excuse me."

Her aunt's mouth gaped as Shelby brushed passed her on the way to the bar. She'd probably pay for that remark later, but it'd been worth it to see the look on her aunt's face.

Shelby ordered two beers and while she waited, scanned the crowd again for Greg. She heard him but couldn't see him, so she accepted her beers and made her way toward his voice. Showtime.

Ignoring the voice in her head that laughed at her, like Nick had about Greg only wanting to play football with her, she powered her feet forward. Suddenly the crowd parted and there he was. Smiling and laughing with . . . Tiffany. Again? The woman was a leech.

Before she could decide what to do, someone called out, "Hey, Shelby, looking good." Ben, one of the neighborhood guys she'd grown up with—and Greg's best friend, held out his hand.

"I'd be glad to take that extra beer off your hands. It looks kinda heavy." He shot her a naughty grin just as he always had. A bad boy to the bone, that one. She'd borrowed many of Ben's antics as a kid for Chester.

She thrust the beer out to him. Greg had a full one anyway. "Too lazy to get your own? You haven't changed much have you, Senator Wright?"

He laughed. "That's why I ran for Senate. That way I'd only have to work once every six years, at reelection time. So, what's new with you, Shelby? Found the man of your dreams or are you still pining after Greg?"

Shelby grabbed his arm and pulled him aside. "If you don't want your wife to know about how you cheated on her during college, I'd keep it down." Ben had been spying on her and Jo during one of their many sleepovers at Jo's house when they were in high school. He'd overheard a conversation about Shelby's love for Greg and he'd made her life a living hell for months. She'd made a point to find dirt on him and was still not above using it.

Ben scowled. "We weren't married yet."

Shelby took a deep drink, pleased she'd rattled him. "No, but you were engaged. And I imagine it'd still upset her to learn it was with her best friend."

"Okay, truce. Geez Shelby, promise you'll never run against me for my seat. I wouldn't have a chance." Then he beamed his wicked but charming grin at her again before he tapped his bottle against hers. "I never told him, you know."

"I don't believe you, Mr. Smoke and Mirrors."

He took a long pull from his beer. "Greg always won at everything when we were kids. I hated he'd beat me to you too, so I never told him, *Summer Sinclair.*" He held her gaze for a moment before he added, "My kid loves your books by the way."

A chill raced up her spine at the way he'd said her pen name. She'd never known he'd liked her when they were young, and it felt a little creepy. "I'd be happy to sign a book for him. But, now I've got to go find Jo. See ya."

"Oh, no you don't." His hand slipped around her upper arm as he whispered, "That hot outfit tells me you're a woman on a mission tonight, so let's go. I want to see Greg's tongue fall out."

Before she could protest, Ben dragged her toward Greg. Tiffany saw them and her frown deepened with each of their advancing steps.

Ben pushed her forward. "Look who I found, Greg."

Greg smiled warmly, then leaned down to lay a soft kiss on Shelby's cheek. "Hey, Shelby." She begged for his gorgeous blue eyes to gaze at all the places she'd hoped, but they stayed locked firmly on her face. "Too bad for the rain, huh? I was looking forward to reestablishing our neighborhood record." Then he turned toward Ben, "Right, buddy?"

Ben's lips tilted into one of his slimy smiles. "We'll have to do that real soon. But we'd probably bore Tiffany to death if we start talking football."

Tiffany flashed a fake smile and batted her eyes at Greg, "Not at all. I just adore football. Especially our Broncos."

Tiffany was one of those women Nick talked about on the way to the country club. Pretending to like football. "So who's your favorite player on the team?" Hah! Take that, Big Chest. If Tiffany's eyes had been laser beams, Shelby would have been disintegrated. "The quarterback, of course."

Ben laughed. "Mine too. But your glass is empty." He slipped his arm around Tiffany's waist. "Let me get you a drink, darling. I'd love to hear your views on the cheerleaders' outfits. I think they're a little snug, myself." He sent Shelby a wink before he left her alone with Greg.

Shelby's mouth went dry and her mind blanked. She, of all people, who had memorized every conversation starter known to man, had nothing. Luckily, Greg saved her.

"So, I hear the writing's going very well, and Jo says your matchmaking business is growing. But do you miss working for your uncle?"

"Nope. I'm considerably poorer at the moment, but I love what I'm doing. How about you? What are your plans now that you're home?" Well that was lame. She needed to flirt with him, not ask the same questions his parents probably asked him.

"I've just accepted a job and I start tomorrow. I'm the new guy, so I'll get the crappy shifts in the ER but it'll be a real change to work in a modern, well equipped hospital instead of the jungle."

"I can imagine. But I'll bet the native girls were sad to see you leave. None of them captured your heart, huh?" That was better.

He laughed. "A few tried, but I outran them." He paused and took a pull from his beer bottle. "I thought you might've had something going on with that Nick guy, but Jo tells me you're between men at the moment?"

"Nick? No we're just . . . friends." Although a friend had never kissed her like Nick had in his Porsche.

"Good. He reminded me of your last boyfriend, what was his name?"

"Ryan?"

"Yeah. I never liked that guy. You're special Shelby, and you should hold out for just the right man."

She always had, and she was looking right at him. "That's my intention." She smiled and stared deeply into his eyes hoping he'd take the hint. But he seemed oblivious to her charms, as usual.

So, on to plan B. "Hey, I was wondering if you'd like to watch the game on Sunday in my uncle's box? We have plenty of room."

His face lit up. "That'd be great. What time should I meet you there?"

She needed her bat so she could knock some sense into him. How dense could Greg be? "We could ride together if you want. Save on parking?"

"Great idea. But I don't have a car yet, I'll have to borrow one. I can't make up my mind between a hybrid, or to go all electric. It's all about the environment, right?"

Shelby smiled, thinking of how Nick would claim it's all about speed. "Yeah. So why don't I pick you up? Then you can drive my new Prius to the game and see what you think of it. Twelve thirty work?"

Someone called out Greg's name so he lifted a finger to signal he'd be right there. "That'd be great. I'm sorry to cut this short. We'll catch up at the game. Just like old times, right?" He kissed her cheek again. "Bye."

"Bye. See you, Sunday." Shelby's heart sank. Their old times were "just friends" times. Was she going to have to strip naked and do a pole dance for him to notice her?

No, that'd be dumb. He might go screaming in the opposite direction at the sight of her legs.

It was early yet, but maybe she should just call it a night. Everyone wanted Greg's attention and her ten minutes were up.

Shelby found Jo, who wasn't ready to leave and said she'd find a ride, so Shelby started for home.

Maybe her outfit wasn't as killer as she thought? Or maybe Greg went for a more conservative look? She needed advice. From a guy. She knew just who to call.

That's what Nick got for being her "friend."

※

Nick rubbed his forehead as he crunched the blurry numbers on his laptop. His neck and back ached and his throat had been sore all day. And he was freezing even though he wore thick socks and sweats. Maybe he'd go upstairs and find a blanket so he could stay warm while he finished his report. He'd compiled all the things he'd learned from Shelby's business model but hadn't given it to his sister yet, telling himself he might learn more on his next date. But the truth was, he'd been putting it off because he felt like such a shit for spying on Shelby. It was killing him worse every day. Maybe he could find a way to get Shelby and Lori to combine their client lists without revealing his spying. The data clearly showed they'd both benefit from that. But how?

When the phone rang, he grimaced. The shrill tone triggered an even more intense pounding in his head as he glanced at the screen. "Hi, Mom."

"Hi, honey. What's wrong?"

Matching Mr. Right

How the hell could his mother tell he felt like garbage from two words? "Bad headache. What's up?"

"Your voice sounds scratchy. I hope you're not getting the flu. I hear it's a rough one with a really high fever."

Nick laid the back of his hand on his forehead. How could it feel so hot when he was freezing? But he never got the flu. "I'll be fine in the morning. What's going on?"

"I wanted to ask a favor. But if you're not feeling well . . ."

"Mom. Stop! What is it?"

She sighed. "You always snap like that when you're sick. We'll talk about it later. I'm going to be near your house tomorrow morning for my yoga class, so I'll stop by and check on you. If you're not there, then I'll assume you're better, and then I'll take measurements for the new curtains I'm making for you."

"I don't need new curtains." Those damned designer curtains currently hanging in his living room had cost him a fortune. "Tell me what the favor is."

"Those curtains are hideous, Nick. I've been telling you that since you built that monstrosity. Why you went and had it decorated professionally when I could have helped you for free is beyond me. So, I'll use my key and either see you in the morning or I won't. Feel better. Love you, goodbye."

"Love you too." Nick tossed his phone aside. Maybe she was right. His curtains were sort of ugly.

He plodded upstairs and found a blanket and then grabbed a pillow off his bed. After dumping everything on the couch, he powered down his laptop. His head hurt too much to be productive anyway. Maybe he'd watch some television. But first he should probably eat something. He hadn't had anything since lunch.

He glanced at the kitchen and sighed. Chicken noodle soup was the only thing that sounded good, but he didn't have any.

He could call his mom back. She'd bring him soup, but then she'd want to stay and fuss over him.

He'd just skip dinner.

He turned on the television and flipped through the channels. After settling on whatever was playing on ESPN, he got up and put more logs on the fire. His teeth chattered he was so cold.

When his phone rang again he hoped it was his mom so he could ask her to bring him some soup after all. He probably did have the flu.

The screen showed Shelby's name, so he poked the little green button and said, "It's early. I thought you were supposed to be wooing Mr. Wonderful tonight at his big welcome-home bash. Was that a bust?"

"Nope, we have a date on Sunday. We're going to the game. But why does your voice sound so funny? Been screaming at the peons at work?"

"I think I have the flu."

"Or, maybe Lisa cast a voodoo spell on you?"

He laughed. "No, and you owe me because I probably caught the bug at *your* restaurant yesterday. I'll take payment in chicken soup or I'll have to sue. Your choice."

"I thought you never got sick, tough guy."

"The clock's ticking. What's it going to be? The soup or my lawyer?"

"Because I was smart enough to get a flu shot, my immune system is impervious to your nasty germs, so you're in luck. I'll run by the café. Do you own a thermometer?"

"No. But I don't need that, just soup. And maybe an éclair."

"I have to stop by the drugstore anyway, so I'll get you some supplies. I have your address from your application, so what's this month's secret gate code to gain entrance to your exclusive, snooty enclave?"

"Your family developed this subdivision, Shelby."

"Not my family, me. It was my project. And what's your point?"

He'd nearly forgotten Shelby had a master's degree in business and used to work for her uncle. Somehow he couldn't picture her being happy doing anything other than what she did now. It must've taken a lot of courage to leave and pursue her dreams.

"You should probably thank me for all that commission you must've made when I wrote that big check for the lot. The code's pound four-two-three."

"Jo'll thank you. It's what I used to invest in her café. See you in a bit."

"'Kay." He closed his dry, burning eyes, laid his aching head onto the back of the couch, and smiled. Shelby hadn't hesitated for a moment to come to his rescue. And if she wanted to stay and fuss over him for a while, he might just have to let her.

10

> "Chester thought taking a sick day off from school would be fun. But it was icky and boring."
> *Chester's Sick Day*

Shelby kicked Nick's front door with her foot as she juggled the bags of sickroom supplies in her arms.

When the huge wooden door swung open, Nick stood before her in gray sweats, thick socks, his hair standing on end, and he still looked cute. It was downright ridiculous.

His eyebrows spiked. "Damn, Shelby. I bet Greg didn't stand a chance once he saw you in that."

Okay, that answered that question. But now she was even more confused and needed his help. "All part of the plan."

She passed by him and then tilted her head in wonder. She'd never guess his furnishings would be so elegant. He must've hired an interior decorator. "Nice. But I hate the curtains."

"I've been hearing that a lot lately." Nick crawled onto a barstool at the granite countertop in the kitchen and frowned as she unloaded her bags. "What's all this crap?"

"I've got nighttime liquid, daytime liquid, Popsicles, and ibuprofen." She dug into the next bag. "Sports drinks to stay hydrated, and what all ailing men need, *Sports Illustrated*. Swimsuit edition."

Nick grunted and laid his forehead on top of his folded arms. "Just soup, Shelby!"

"That too, Mr. Grouchy. I'll nuke it for you."

After she put the soup into the stainless steel microwave, she opened the new digital thermometer. Yanking a handful of his thick hair, she lifted his head up. When he opened his mouth to protest, she stuck it in.

"Geez, Nurse Ratched. Take it easy, will you?" he mumbled around the thermometer.

Shelby laughed as she pulled out the éclairs and the cookies she'd thrown in at the last minute. When she opened his refrigerator to put the éclairs away, she gasped. "Seriously, Nick? It's like a college dorm room fridge. How many different kinds of leftover fast-food containers can we stuff into an oversized Subzero?" She opened a box and gagged at the green fuzzy stuff inside.

She gathered boxes in her arms to throw them away when he barked, "Leave it. I'll do that later."

"Fine." She tossed them all back in.

When the thermometer beeped, she grabbed it before he could. "Holy crap, Nick. It's a hundred and three! You really are sick." Poor baby. She regretted being so abrupt with him earlier. "Have you taken anything?"

He shivered as he laid his head back down. "No."

"We need to get that fever down." She laid the bowl of soup in front of him and unwrapped the sourdough rolls she'd brought along. Then she measured out the medicine and poured him a glass of water. "Take these first . . . please."

He obeyed without complaint for a change and then slowly started in on his soup. After a few bites he laid his spoon down. "It's too hot. Maybe I want something cold?"

"That's what I figured." She grabbed one of the strawberry Popsicles she'd brought. "Try this."

When he placed it into his mouth, he sighed. "That's good."

While he ate, she climbed up next to him at the bar. "In my experience, there are two kinds of sick men. A) the ones who tell you to go away because they hate to be coddled and B) the ones who tell you to go away because they hate to be coddled but don't really mean it. Which are you?"

Nick finished off his Popsicle and frowned. "Somewhere between A and B."

"Right. No simple A or B for you." She hopped down and put the leftover soup away, then wiped down the counters. "Want me to stay and watch a movie with you?"

"I guess. But no chick flicks."

"I think the Romance Channel is running a marathon tonight." Not really, but it was too perfect a teasing opportunity to pass up.

"Dammit, Shelby!" He moved to the living room and flopped onto the huge leather couch. "I can't take one of those tonight."

Dammit Shelby seemed to be his favorite moniker for her. Strangely, it was growing on her.

"Like you could take one of those movies any night? You haven't got a romantic bone in your body."

"Proud of it."

Shaking her head, she grabbed the remote, slipped off her boots and settled in on the matching loveseat. They were big, oversized couches. Man-sized. So big and deep, Shelby's feet didn't touch the floor when she sat up, so she tucked them under her and settled back into the butter-soft cushions. As she flipped through the channels, Nick wrapped himself up in his blanket, but it didn't seem to have any effect on his shivering.

She searched for something they'd both like because she felt sorry for him. He had to be miserable with that high a fever.

When his shaking became more violent, he snapped, "I need your body heat!"

Her finger froze over the remote. "And just how would I provide that particular service, Your Highness?"

"Come over here and lay beside me."

When she hesitated while trying to decide if that was a guy move to get his hands on her, he said, "I've got a fever of a hundred and three. It's not like I'm going to molest you!"

He had a point. But he didn't have to yell about it.

She moved to his couch and slipped under the blanket. With her back to his chest she tried to maintain a respectful distance, but he laid his hand on her stomach and pulled her against his big body. It wasn't a hardship spooning with Nick, he was built. But he wasn't Greg, so she should probably try not to enjoy it so much.

To distract herself, she flipped through the channels as poor Nick shivered violently behind her. After a few minutes, his shivers quieted and he sighed.

Her head was tucked under his on a pillow that held his yummy scent, and she was all warm and cozy, so when *Raiders of The Lost Ark* showed up on the guide she asked, "How about—"

"Yup."

Tossing the remote on his coffee table, she settled in, grinning in anticipation. It was one of her favorite movies.

While the beginning credits rolled, she remembered why she'd called him in the first place. It might even make it easier to ask because he was too sick to tease her—much. "Nick, my outfit tonight screams 'please sleep with me' doesn't it?"

He grunted. "Greg still just wants to play football with you?"

"Sort of. What do you think I should do to make it clear I want more?"

"Back up. What did you guys talk about at the party? Did he ask if you're seeing anyone?"

She rewound their conversation in her mind. "He mentioned he knew I was between men. And that at first he thought you and I were together. He was glad we weren't because he didn't like you because you reminded him of my last boyfriend."

Nick's body stiffened behind her. "He's an ass, Shelby. Find someone else. You could have any guy you want."

"But I think I want this one," she whispered.

He blew out a long breath. "Kiss him. You're really good at it."

She turned her head to see his face. He had to be kidding, right? "Don't tease Nick, I'm serious."

"I'm not teasing. You are." He tightened his hold on her as he shivered again. "Now can we please just watch the movie? All this talking is making me wish I'd told you I was a solid type A patient so I could have some peace and quiet."

"Fine." Shelby snuggled a little closer and smiled. A guy like Nick thought she was a good kisser? Wow.

After a few minutes of reliving their last kiss in his Porsche, she whispered, "You're a good kisser too, Nick."

His hand found one of hers, then he wove their fingers together. "If I didn't feel like I'd just been hit by a dump truck, I'd show you what else I'm good at. You want a rain check?"

"Even when sick, men are such dogs. Shut up and watch the movie."

When his low chuckle reverberated off her back, she grinned and tucked their entwined hands under her chin. Why was it so nice to hold Nick's hand? She'd never felt that comforting connection with anyone before.

So *did* she want a rain check?

The way he kissed, and with that smoking hot body, she could only imagine how good he'd be in bed. But sex was all he wanted, so it wasn't worth thinking about.

But it was tough not to. As she watched the familiar movie, her lids grew heavy so she closed her eyes.

After what seemed like a short ten-minute nap, Shelby blinked her eyes open. A different movie played on the big screen. She reached above her head and felt Nick's forehead. Still burning up.

Her phone showed enough time had passed so he could take more medicine. She'd dose him up with the nighttime stuff to knock him out and then be on her way.

When she tried to slip out of his embrace, his arms clamped tightly around her. "Stay!"

"I'm not a dog you can order around, Nick."

"I feel like crap. Please?"

She knew the feeling. When she'd gotten sick after moving in with her aunt and uncle, the only one who ever checked on her was the cook. She'd laid in bed feeling miserable all by herself. "Okay. But I need to borrow a T-shirt and some sweats. I'm not sleeping in my jeans." Or her push up bra. It was doing its job a little too well and killing her.

"My bedroom dresser, bottom right-hand drawer."

"Fine, but just know I have a tendency to snoop."

Shelby went to the kitchen to get Nick's medicine along with a sports drink. She texted Jo and told her she wouldn't be home, and then after badgering Nick until he drank every bit of the sports drink, she climbed the stairs.

At the top she turned to the right and opened a door. It wasn't the master bedroom, but one a princess could call home. It held a pink canopy bed and shelves stuffed with books and toys. Must be Emily's room when she spent the night.

Too cute.

She turned out the light, closed the door, and then walked the opposite direction down a long hallway. When she opened the door at the end and crossed the threshold, she smiled. Talk about nice. The master bedroom had rich hunter-green walls, beautiful cherry wood furniture, a huge bed—of course—and sage-colored carpet. And because she had to pee, she checked out his bathroom. It was equally large, with a deep jet tub and a shower that could hold ten people.

The closet was one any woman would envy and was scary-neat and organized. All his shoes stood in straight lines on shelves, and his neatly folded ties were grouped by color. His formal wear and suits were on one wall and his casual clothes on the other. Geez, she'd never known a man could be so tidy. But not when it came to his fridge, evidently.

She found some sweats and a beer T-shirt and then changed into them. Even after pulling the drawstrings on the sweats as tight as she could, she still had to hold them up at the waist while she snooped in his bedside drawers. Was Nick the naughty-tools-and-gadgets type?

Nope. Nothing unusual, just a few popular mystery paperbacks—mostly unread if the bookmarks were any indication—lip balm, a mini flashlight, a pen, and some paper. Digging deeper, way on the bottom, she found two condoms.

Boring. But nice to know he wasn't a freak or anything since she was about to sleep with him. Sort of.

Nick's voice drifted up the stairs, "Stop whatever you're doing and get back down here!"

She laughed and ran to the other side to see if Beth had left anything more exciting. When she opened the drawer it was empty. He said she never spent the night. He'd been telling the truth about Beth after all.

Shelby went downstairs and straight to the kitchen. "You're single again Nick, so two condoms, that are probably old, aren't going to cut it. I'll put them on the grocery list for you."

"You went through my nightstand? What if I'd had whips and handcuffs in there?"

"It would have been a lot less boring, that's for sure." She wrote "condoms" in extra-large print on the top of the empty grocery list attached by a magnet to the fridge. Hopefully when he was feeling better he'd get his sense of humor back and it'd make him smile.

Nick had a great smile.

Shelby turned out the lights and made sure the screen around the still-burning fire was extra secure. Then she slipped under the blanket, snuggled up against all of his glorious muscles, and laid a soft kiss on his hot forehead. "Behave."

"Now who's boring?" Nick pulled her closer and shivered. "'Nite, Shelby."

"Goodnight, Grump."

She closed her eyes and drifted back to sleep.

⁂

Sometime deep into the night, Shelby's thrashing woke Nick. The fire had flared so the living room was unnaturally bright. Shelby mumbled about running to get away. Should he wake her?

Then she sat straight up. "Fire! We have to get out!" She pulled on his arm. "We have to go, Nick. Now!"

"It's just the fireplace. You were dreaming. Look."

She turned with widened eyes and stared at the fireplace for a moment before she closed them tight against the tears that leaked out the edges.

Her fight against the tears killed him. Pulling her against his chest, he tucked her head under his chin. "You're safe, Shelby."

She wrapped her arms around him and held on tight as her whole body shook. "Sorry. I still get dreams about the fire sometimes. I'm so pathetic, I've never even used my fireplace and I don't allow candles in the house."

"No, that makes sense." He laid a kiss on the top of her head as jolt of pain stabbed his heart at the thought of Shelby, trapped in a burning house, trying to save her sister. "Do you want a drink of water or something?"

She shook her head. "I'm fine. Sorry I woke you."

"It's okay." He laid another soft kiss on her forehead. "Sweet dreams."

After a while her breathing finally steadied and she fell back asleep. Only then would he allow himself to do the same. As he thought about her story, something still bugged him about the fire. So what if she'd left the burner on? That alone wouldn't necessarily start a fire, unless she'd left a towel nearby or something. What if there had been faulty wiring or something entirely unrelated. Would they think to tell Shelby, who was a child sick in the hospital, and who'd just lost her family? There must be a police or fire report somewhere to confirm what had happened. But he wouldn't want to upset her by

Matching Mr. Right

dredging it all up, especially if her theory was true. So maybe he'd find a way to look into that without her knowing. He owed her that at least for deceiving her.

～

Sunlight flowing through Nick's twelve-foot-high windows assaulted Shelby's eyelids. She blinked her eyes open and found herself still draped over Nick, his chest a fine pillow. She hadn't moved since he wrapped her up tight and held her after the dream. The only difference was his hand had slipped under her loose sweats and cupped around her butt. Because she'd worn a thong, it was bare skin he held.

"Nick?" She lifted her hand to feel his forehead. Still hot.

He moaned, but didn't wake, so she poked him in the ribs. "Nick!"

His eyes jerked open. "What?"

"Move your hand."

He gave her bottom a gentle squeeze. "Nice."

Before she could snap at him, his hand slipped under her T-shirt. When his fingernails softly raked in long, slow strokes up and down her back, she arched like a cat.

His chest rumbled under hers. "Shelby likes her back scratched."

"Doesn't everyone?" She closed her eyes and fought the sigh that wanted to escape. "Sorry about the nightmare last night."

How embarrassing that he'd seen her like that. It probably wasn't normal to still be such a freak about fire. But he'd been so patient and sweet, holding her tightly all night, making her feel safe.

There it was again, that sweet side he hid so well.

Nick murmured, "Thanks for staying." His long fingers, still gliding smoothly up and down her back, had just found the side of her bare breast when the sound of pots and pans rattling in the kitchen stopped his movement.

"Someone's in your kitchen? Does Beth have a key?" Awkward. Especially because Beth was her client now.

Nick's fingers started up their pattern against her sensitive skin again and it sent a shiver down her spine. "Only my mom has a key."

"Your mom? Do you think she saw us?" She threw back the blanket, hopped off of Nick, and moved to the loveseat.

"I'm sure she did. We'd be hard to miss from the front door. Who cares?"

"I'll bet she couldn't miss your grocery list either."

His head whipped toward hers. "I thought you were kidding about that. Dammit, Shelby!"

Before she could escape, his mom walked into the living room. "Good morning, you two." She laid a kiss on Nick's forehead and winced. "That's some fever, sweetheart."

Nick grunted.

"Morning, Mrs. Caldwell. This looks bad, but it isn't what you think."

Before his mom could respond, Nick said, "Shelby's like Buddy."

"Well, that makes sense."

Not to Shelby. "Who's Buddy?"

Nick's mom smiled sweetly. "Nick had a golden retriever named Buddy when he was a kid. Buddy always seemed to know when someone in the family was sad or not feeling well, and he'd crawl up next to one of us and cuddle until we felt better." She stared into Nick's eyes for a moment before she turned and stared into Shelby's. "Nick really loved that dog, Shelby."

Shelby's stomach took a dive at the implication in his mother's voice. "Ah . . . okay. Well, I should get going." She stood and hitched her pants up. "So, it's time for his medicine again, and don't trust anything in his fridge except the soup and the éclairs. I left some cookies for him on the counter." She held on to her pants with both hands and started for the stairs. "Oh, and don't try to clean his fridge out—even though it's a biohazard—because he wants to do that himself. He'd never dream of asking his *mother* to do it."

"I'm sitting right here, Shelby!" Nick growled.

She shot him a grin before she zipped up the stairs.

❧

Nick glanced at his mom. "You saw her car out front and still used your key instead of ringing the doorbell?"

His mom chuckled. "I didn't know the car belonged to Shelby. And it's parked in the street, not your driveway. But never in my wildest did I think I'd find you and Shelby cuddled up on the couch."

"We're just friends." He ran a hand down his face, digging deep for patience.

"That's probably why you need those condoms on your grocery list so badly." His mother sat beside him. "It's written in bold letters."

He'd kill Shelby for making him have a discussion about condoms with his mother. "Shelby did that to annoy me. In case you haven't noticed, it's her mission in life."

"Mmmm." She nodded slowly. "Yes, it's always best to snuggle with the ones who annoy us the most. But it was nice of her to stay and help. Are you hungry?"

He ignored her sarcasm. "A little. Shelby brought Popsicles. Maybe I'll have one of those."

"She brought you Popsicles?" His mother's eyes sparked with delight. Not a good sign. Before his mom could continue her torment, Shelby joined them again.

"Okay, he's all yours, Mrs. Caldwell. I'll wish you luck. He's the crankiest sick person I've ever met. But I'm sure you already knew that, knowing him his whole life and all."

His mother laughed, the traitor. "He was probably on his best behavior for *you*, Shelby."

"I hope for your sake that's not true." Shelby moved in front of him and laid her cool hands on the sides of his face, lifting it up. Then her lips tilted into one of those cute smiles he'd seen her beam at kids. "But in his weakened state, a few moments of sweetness managed to escape. Feel better, Grump." She planted a noisy kiss on his forehead he wished had been on his mouth, then she turned to his mom. "Bye, Mrs. Caldwell."

"Bye, honey."

After Shelby left, he turned toward his mom's smirking face. "Stop. We're just friends."

"Uh, huh. And I'm the Easter Bunny."

Since when had his mom become such a smartass?

11

> "Chester didn't want to accept an apology from the kid who stole his football, but the teacher made them shake hands anyway."
> **Chester Tries to Forgive**

Shelby admired the beautiful orchid in the center of the kitchen table at Nick's mother's house. Emily had texted—or had someone do it for her—before school asking if they were still going to write a book together about being in the hospital. No way she could say no to that. "This is so pretty. But I hear they're hard to keep alive."

Mrs. Caldwell, who had insisted Shelby call her Linda, smiled. "I enjoy the challenge, but haven't had one in years. Nick's father sent it. He's been acting strangely lately." Linda sat across from Shelby and passed a plate of still-warm-from-the-oven cookies toward her. "Now that I think of it, it's been ever since I started dating a younger man."

Linda took a bite of cookie, then her eyes grew wide. "Nick doesn't know I date, so I'd appreciate it if you wouldn't say anything about that, Shelby."

"No, of course not." Nick didn't know his mother dated? Something was up. She'd have to explore that later.

The front door opened and a deep voice called out, "Anyone home?"

Linda frowned. "We're in the kitchen, Ed."

Nick's father walked in and laid his hands on Linda's shoulders. "You got the orchid. Hello, Shelby."

"Hi, Mr. Caldwell. It's nice to see you again."

Linda's brows scrunched. "Thank you for the orchid, but I still can't figure out why you sent it. Maybe you should get a physical. It's like you've had a stroke and you forgot to act like the ass you've been for the past twenty years."

Shelby stifled a laugh.

He said, "We used to always have one in the house, so I wanted to buy you another."

"That confirms it. You have had a stroke, Edward." Linda hopped up and scooped cookies off of the pan. "Don't you remember why I always had an orchid in the house? It reminded me of our Hawaiian wedding, and how in love we were back then. When you left, I tossed the one I had out, just like you did with me and the kids, and I vowed to never have another!" Blinking back her tears, Linda turned her back to him and pretended to clean her already spotless kitchen counters.

Things were getting way too personal for Shelby's taste.

Nick's dad said, "Maybe I wanted to see if we could make an orchid grow again, Linda."

Deciding it best to leave the two of them alone at such a crucial moment, Shelby stood and headed for the door, only to run into a familiar, hard chest.

Nick's big, hard chest.

His hands slipped to her waist to steady her. "What are you doing here? And where's Lori?"

Matching Mr. Right

"I have no idea where your sister is." Why would Nick ask her that?

He glanced around the kitchen and when he saw his father, a scowl darkened his face.

His parents' discussion came to an abrupt halt. They all stared at each other as tension hung thick in the air.

She felt like someone should say something, so she looked up at Nick. "What are *you* doing here? Shouldn't you be home in bed? Aren't you still sick?"

"I stayed home from work but I'm bored out of my skull. Mom mentioned she was baking cookies today and she made a batch for me. I thought I'd save her a trip." He tugged her closer. "So, why are you here Shelby?"

Before she could answer, an excited six-year-old bounded through the door. Emily sent her backpack flying onto a chair before she launched herself at the back of Shelby's legs, wrapping them up tightly. "Hi, Shelby. I'm ready to write!"

She slipped out of Nick's embrace then lifted Emily up to her eye level. "Me too. Want to grab a snack before we start? Your grandma made some yummy cookies."

She glanced at Nick over Emily's head. When he sent Emily a cute proud-uncle smile it warmed her heart.

But then Nick spotted the orchid and his face turned to stone. Picking it up, he asked his mom, "Where did this come from? I haven't seen one of these in the house since I was a kid."

Nick's mom glanced at Edward, who in turn looked at Shelby. Geez, what was with these people? She wasn't even part of the family. Why were they looking at her? But then a thought struck her.

Passing Emily off to Mrs. Caldwell, she turned to Nick and plastered on a smile. "It came for your mom today. From a secret admirer."

Nick scowled as he searched the plant for a card. "My mom hates orchids." He started toward the trash with it, but Linda laid her hand on his arm and stopped him.

"But this one is kind of pretty, Nick." She shifted Emily on her hip before she took the plant from him. Then she glanced at Edward. "I'm finding my tastes are changing as I get older. How about you, Ed?"

Edward smiled. "Absolutely."

Nick frowned and looked at his mother as if she'd lost her marbles. "Whatever. Bye, Mom." He started toward the door, and ignoring his father's presence, said, "I'll see you later Short Stuff."

"Bye, Uncle Nick," Emily mumbled around a bite of cookie.

Nick's mom called out, "Don't you want your cookies?"

Ignoring his mother, Nick slipped his hand around Shelby's arm. Impersonating a caveman again, he tugged her through the mudroom and then outside with him. Before she could ask what he was doing, he backed her up against the garage. Sliding his big hands slowly along her cheeks and then into her hair, he tilted her face and laid his soft, warm lips on hers.

It wasn't a gentle kiss, but one filled with heat and frustration. And so much desire she feared her brain cells would never be the same. When his thigh slipped between her legs and he pressed his chest against hers she was afraid she'd spontaneously combust. The man flipped a switch in her she never knew was there.

She lifted her hands into his thick hair, pulling him even closer, and a deep moan rumbled from his chest.

She should put an end to the kiss, but her ability to reason had apparently booked a cruise to Antarctica. The bad girl she always hid so deeply within kind of hoped her frozen brain cells would stay right where they were for just a while longer.

Nick's warm hands took their time exploring her body before heading south and finally reaching their destination—her rear end. He gave her bottom a gentle squeeze. Then he slowly moved his lips to the sensitive skin in front of her ear. When he laid soft kisses there, sending skitters of lust up her spine, a blaze of desire raced through her body. Now her brain cells weren't anywhere near Antarctica—they were smoldering in Hades.

Nick nearly drove her over the edge as he trailed hot kisses along her jaw and then teased the corner of her mouth. She wanted his lips back on hers, *pronto*.

At the sound of her frustrated moan, he abruptly pulled his mouth away, blinking as if he suddenly remembered they were outside of his mother's house instead of in a bedroom where they could finish what he'd started. Good thing his brain cells seemed to still be working, because hers had committed hara-kiri long ago.

With her hands still buried in his soft hair, she gazed into his smoldering blue eyes, waiting for an explanation. When none came, and he seemed perfectly content to stare right back at her with a sexy little grin on his lips, she whispered, "What was that for?"

"Just felt like it." He shrugged. "It's nice you're going to write the book with Em. Bye." He kissed her again so softly her heart melted, then he turned and walked away.

She closed her eyes and let her head fall back against the hard siding. She wanted Nick, that was obvious to all the parts of her body that made her a female, but worse, she'd come to care for him. A lot.

So what was wrong with ignoring her raging hormones and just being his friend? If she let her traitorous body have its way they'd be lovers and probably have a few great weeks, but then he'd move on. Her already scarred heart, one that had never been the same after the loss of her family, couldn't handle any more lacerations. But every time she kissed Nick she wanted him even more, dammit!

She turned to go back inside to get started on her new Chester book with Emily.

Better to forget Nick's hot kisses and take the safe path with Greg. Maybe she'd get lucky and Greg would make her brains fry when he finally kissed her too.

Or at least sizzle a little.

She could live with that.

When she walked into the kitchen, Emily had crumbs on her chin, smeared chocolate on her pudgy little fingers, and a big grin on her cherubic face. No wonder Nick was so smitten with his niece. She was an adorable kid. And one more reason to pursue Greg. He wanted little Emilys and Nick didn't.

While Emily finished up her snack, Shelby turned to check on Nick's parents. They stood side-by-side, leaning against the kitchen counter with matching smug smiles on their lips.

Confused by their self-satisfied looks, Shelby asked, "Did you guys work everything out?"

Mrs. Caldwell chuckled. "No, our situation isn't one so easily solved. But thanks for distracting Nick, Shelby. You really took one for the team out there—and boy, did you sell it!"

She swiveled her head. The window in front of the sink provided a clear view of where she'd just been standing with Nick.

Crap, crap, crap! They must've seen the whole thing.

Cornered, Shelby shrugged and tried her best to stave off the blush she feared was creeping up her neck. "Nick still isn't feeling well. Just wanted to keep the peace." Scooping Emily up, Shelby made a run for it. "Let's go write a book, Monkey-Brains."

※

Nick was about to do something he thought he'd never do. Ask his father for a favor. He'd been thinking about Shelby and the fire ever since she'd spent the night with him a few days ago. That, and he'd decided to delete the data he'd gathered from Shelby and try to help his sister some other way.

He owed Shelby whether she knew it yet or not. If that meant involving his father then he'd suck it up and get it done.

He walked into his father's opulent suite of offices located in the trendiest part of town, and the receptionist told him to go straight in. The cost of the furniture and paintings on the walls in the lobby alone would buy his mother a new car.

When he opened his father's office door, his dad stood. "Hi, Nick. This is a pleasant surprise."

Nick closed the door behind him and forced his feet to move forward. His father held out his hand so Nick reluctantly shook it. After all, he was the one asking for a favor.

Was it the lingering fever, or was it overly hot in his dad's office? Nick loosened his tie a little. It was hard to breathe.

After he sat down, his father surprised him by rounding his desk and sitting in the chair beside him. "I'm glad you stopped by. I wanted to talk to you at your mom's yesterday, but you left too quickly. I should have made my intentions clear the other night at the auction rather than taken you by surprise. But Mom said you guys had fun at the game?"

His father had called three times, but he hadn't bothered to return them. Lori made a good point about how the country club set didn't care about being good parents. Maybe he had jumped to the wrong conclusion. A sliver of guilt crept into his gut. "Yeah, it turned out to be a fun night. Emily enjoyed it as well, so . . . thanks."

His father smiled. "Good. It's nice to see Emily smiling again since her father died. Mom says you've really stepped in and helped, so thank you for that."

"It's no trouble. Em's a great kid."

"She is. Mom and I worry about Lori though, and wish she'd try to get out more. She's really taking Joe's death hard. I can't blame her for it, but all she does is work and take care of Emily. And she won't take a nickel from us. Your mother even offered to buy her a house and told her she could live there for whatever rent she could afford until she was back on her feet. But Lori wouldn't do it."

Nick blinked in confusion. "I offered that too, but how could Mom afford to buy Lori a house?"

His father frowned. "Your mother makes exactly what I do a year, Nick. Half of my earnings go to her. They always have and always will. Just because I screwed up doesn't make me any less responsible for my family."

Half? No respectable divorce lawyer would let himself get screwed like that. It didn't make sense. His father's billings had to be a million a year or more. "Mom lives in the same house she always has, drives a ten-year-old Camry, cleans out her own gutters, and you're telling me she makes six figures a year?"

"Yes. Your mother just doesn't choose to spend her money like I do. You should see her portfolio. It'd make you look like a pauper, Nick. And I know you've done very well for yourself."

So his father hadn't left his mother to hang out to dry like he'd always assumed? She was just being frugal? Whatever. It still didn't excuse his infidelity and asking his kid to lie for him.

"I'm glad to know mom's taken care of. One less worry for me."

"She's not your responsibility Nick, she's mine. And I hope you'll let your mother and I worry about Lori and Emily. Mom tells me you have enough on your plate right now with the women in your life?"

"Mom and Lori are a pain in the ass sometimes, especially when it comes to butting into my personal business."

"I'm afraid that's not something you can change, either. Better to just grin and bear it. Now, what can I do for you? You mentioned you needed help with something?"

Nick hated asking for anything from his dad, but it was probably the quickest way to solve Shelby's mystery. "When Shelby was a child, her family's home caught fire. I know you have private investigators and friends at the police station. Do you think you could find a report that states the origin of the fire?"

"That shouldn't be too difficult." His father stood and then sat behind his desk. Pulling out a yellow legal pad, he said, "Give me the details. Family name, dates, everything you know, and I'll put my best man on it."

"I'd like it as soon as possible and I'll pay whatever—"

His father held up a hand. "No. I'm happy to help. You wouldn't ask if it wasn't important."

Just like that? His dad didn't even ask him why? Could it really be so simple or would he have to pay in some other way later?

No, he'd have to pay. His dad was a ruthless bastard. He should just go. He didn't want to owe the man.

But he owed Shelby. And his dad hadn't hesitated to help.

"Thanks. I appreciate it." He gave his dad the details and got out of there as quickly as he could. His shoulders and neck ached they were so tied up in knots.

He was drenched in stress sweat, so before he climbed into his car, he yanked his suit coat off and then his tie, tossing them onto the passenger seat. Maybe his father *had* changed. Maybe it was time to let it go, just forgive his father and himself the way Shelby needed to forgive herself. Move on.

He slid behind the wheel, put his car into gear, and smiled. Even Lisa the whacky lawyer-turned-witch from his blind date had said he couldn't be happy harboring all that guilt. She also mentioned he was in love with a woman and should pursue her because she'd make him happy. Maybe it was time to let go and be happy again. Was Shelby the woman spooky Lisa had been talking about?

He zipped into traffic and headed toward the café. He was starving after living on Popsicles and chocolate chip cookies for two days. But most of all, he wanted to see Shelby.

She got him. Like no one else.

And she kissed like no one else. Maybe he could wrangle a repeat of that as well.

He dug out his phone and dialed her number.

She picked up after two rings. "Hi, Nick. Are you feeling better or is this another blackmail attempt to gain soup?"

"All recovered. Where are you?"

"Why?"

"I've had a lousy morning, please don't mess with me. Have you had lunch?"

"Recovered, and yet, still grumpy. I have some dating prospects for you, so I need to talk to you anyway. I'm at the café."

"I'll be there in five." He hung up and threw his phone onto the seat beside him.

Shelby sighed and put her phone back into her purse. Why did he always do that? Just hang up when he was done talking. He needed to learn some phone manners.

She dug through the dating advice files on her laptop and found an article on phone etiquette. She'd just forwarded it to Nick's e-mail as he flopped down onto a chair opposite her.

He was obviously upset about something, so she let the phone thing go. "Hi. What sounds good for lunch? I'll go get it from the back and then you can tell me what's going on."

"Meat. I'm starving!"

She laughed. "Of course. Be right back."

While they ate, Nick told her about visiting his father, but she couldn't imagine what would be so compelling that he'd asked his dad for something. Nick said it was a favor for a friend. She hoped that friend understood how big a sacrifice he'd just made for him or her. "Okay, so now you're off-balance because you can't be mad at your dad for one of the things that pissed you off the most. The leaving your mom a pauper thing, right?"

Nick took a big bite of his meatball sub and shrugged.

"So let's break this down. You're still mad at your dad for leaving your mom, making her unhappy, and then ruining your family. And because he asked you to lie to your mother?"

He nodded and took another big bite.

"See the thing is Nick, your mom seems like a really happy person to me. And you have such a nice family it melts my heart, so I'm not sure I can side with you on those two points." She took a bite of her salad. "But your dad was a real jerk to ask you to lie. I'll give you that one. And I know you'll always feel bad for lying to your mom, but she obviously doesn't hold that against you. So if all that's left is your dad being a jerk in the moment he probably realized he was busted . . . you might have to find a way to realize he's just a flawed person. Like, if your mom was an alcoholic, you'd hate her drinking, but you'd never hate *her*. You couldn't."

She wished she could tell Nick how much his dad seemed to have changed. And how hope had filled his mother's eyes for a brief moment when Edward had suggested they repair their relationship.

Nick frowned as he drained his iced tea. "What pisses me off most, Shelby, is what you said makes perfect sense. And I think I'm ready to move on. So why can't I just let it go?"

"I don't know. Maybe you feel like if you let it go, stop hating your father, then what he did would be okay? And then you'd be no better than your dad? But from where I'm sitting, you're ten times the man your father is. You don't lie, or use your good looks to get ahead—you work hard for what you want. You don't flirt with or use women, you actually respect them. That's something I would have never guessed the first time I met you. But, too bad for you, because actions speak louder than words."

Nick's right brow winged up and he grinned. "Thanks. But you're wrong. I do flirt, but only with *you*. It just doesn't seem to work."

"It works. A little." She smiled as she sipped her iced tea. "But I'm a sensible woman and am keeping my eye on the goal. You would be a mistake, One-Night Stand Man. Probably a really fun one, but still a mistake."

"Guess I'll have to step up my game." He stood and slid his chair under the table. "Thanks for lunch. Now I want dessert." Nick leaned down, lifted her chin, and then laid a whopper of a kiss on her lips. Heat zipped through her body so fast it left her dizzy. Why did he have to be so good at that?

When he slowly leaned away, he said. "Delicious. See you on Sunday."

Matching Mr. Right

"Sunday?"

"Yeah, Jake invited me to the game, remember? Bye."

She'd forgotten about that. How was she going to make moves on Greg with Nick there distracting all of her hormones? Dammit, Nick!

❦

After Nick's fourth piece of loaded deep-dish pizza, he leaned away from his mother's kitchen table and patted his stomach. "Now that ladies, is what the perfect slice of pizza is all about. I love Friday pizza night the most when it's my turn to pick."

Lori, his mom, and Emily all scrunched up their noses. "I like thin crust better, Uncle Nick."

"No you don't." He poked Emily in the side. "You're just siding with the girls. Whenever you spend the night we always get this kind."

Emily snickered. "Momma says ladies are allowed to change their minds."

"But it doesn't make it any less annoying when you do."

Lori cleared their plates. "Mom, did you know Nick is going to the football game again on Sunday? In Shelby's suite."

"Really?" His mother wiped Emily's mouth and hands. "Well, say hello to her for me."

Nick grunted. "Shelby is going to be there with her date. Prince Charming."

"Shelby knows Prince Charming?" Emily's eyes grew wide.

"No. She just thinks she does." Nick picked up the pizza box and threw it in the trash. "He's not her type. He's like a hippie, surfer, do-gooder, boring person. If there's one thing Shelby's not, it's boring."

Lori slowly nodded. "So, what are you going to do about it? Just stand by and let this dull beatnik have her?"

Nick sat at the table again. "Shelby wants the whole deal. Husband and three little Emilys." Nick gently tugged on one of Emily's curls. "One little Emily's all I can handle."

But he loved Emily. He'd do anything for her. Maybe having his own Emilys wouldn't be so bad? Could he make a real relationship with Shelby work?

Lori's grin turned wicked. "Emily can be a lot for anyone to handle. Maybe she should go along with you to the game? It'd show Shelby how tough it is to be romantic while holding a sticky-fingered kid in her lap. You should definitely get cotton candy."

Emily's head whipped up. "Cotton candy? Please Uncle Nick? Can I go?"

Nick met his sister's mischievous matchmaker's gaze. "You mean I should hang out with the guys and Emily should hang all over Shelby? Gooey fingers and all?"

"I didn't say that. You did. What time will you be picking Em up? No, even better. I'll drop you guys off. Then I'll call and tell you why I can't pick you up, then you'll have to ride home with Shelby and the prince."

"That's not nice, you two." His mom chuckled.

Nick scooped Emily up and held her over his head "Okay little wingman. Do your job by hanging out with Shelby and there may be a trip to the toy store in your future. See you guys Sunday at noon."

Yeah. That plan might just work.

12

> "When monkeys commit the crime, they have to do the time."
> *Chester's Big Scheme*

Shelby walked into her uncle's suite at the football stadium with Greg, her stomach tight with nerves. The car ride over had been a little awkward and quiet at times. But maybe he'd been distracted with checking out her car before he bought one of his own. Hopefully, he'd loosen up after a beer.

Who was she kidding? She was the one who needed that beer. Dating sucked.

She'd considered dressing in something a little cuter like a normal person, but Nick had told her she looked hot in her jersey, so she'd gone with it. She ignored the heat gathering in her gut as she recalled the way Nick's eyes had darkened with desire before he'd told her that.

She and Greg hadn't walked two feet inside her uncle's box before a dark-curly-headed blur ran toward her with open arms. "Hi, Shelby!"

She pried Emily's arms from around her legs and lifted her up. "Hi, Em. I didn't know you were going to be here today." She turned to Greg. "This is one of my biggest fans, and my new writing buddy, Emily Monkey-Brains."

"That's a great name. I'm Greg." He beamed a big smile at Emily.

Just like a little chimp, Emily wrapped her arms around Shelby's neck, her legs around her waist and settled in before she said to Greg, "Uncle Nick calls you Prince Charming. Are you Shelby's boyfriend?"

Nick was a dead man.

Greg sputtered, "Well, um—"

Shelby jumped in before he turned a deeper shade of red. "So, where is your Uncle Nick, honey?"

Emily threw out her hand toward the bar. "With those big guys. They're kinda scary."

"But they're the nicest people ever. Let's go find your uncle."

"Can I sit with you, Shelby?" Emily's lips tilted into a sweet grin.

She glanced at Greg, whose color had faded to almost normal again. "Do you mind?"

Greg shook his head. "No, it's fine. Want a beer?"

God, yes!

"Sure. Thanks." She carried Emily down to the front, hoping Mikey would be there. Maybe he'd brought his Legos. This could be a disaster in the making. And unfortunately, Mikey and his parents weren't there.

After she settled with Emily on her lap, a pair of big hands slipped over her shoulders and gave a gentle squeeze. They certainly weren't Greg's hands. But somehow her heart didn't seem to mind as it kicked into high gear at Nick's soft caress.

His warm breath tickled her ear as he whispered, "Hey, Shelby. Looking *hot*, as always. Emily needs some cotton candy. I'll be right back, okay?"

"No!" She turned to argue the wisdom of that particular treat, but Nick was already headed for the door. She huffed out a breath and closed her eyes. It could be a very long afternoon.

A few moments later Greg slid beside them and handed her a beer. "You used to like Amstel Light, if I recall?"

"I do. Thanks." As she took a long drink, Emily patted her shoulder. "I'm thirsty too, Shelby."

"What can I get for you?" Greg dropped his beer into the cup holder and hopped up again.

That was nice of him. Or maybe he was just happy to be away from Emily and the possibility that another embarrassing question would pop out of her mouth.

Emily scrunched her forehead. "A big orange soda?"

"You got it."

She probably should've suggested he make it a small one, but he'd left too quickly.

A few minutes later Nick returned and sat beside her with a huge cone of cotton candy. Her stomach joined in with the rest of her mutinous body, clenching at the sight of him.

He'd bought a new Bronco's Jersey—that was evident from the price tag peeking out from under the back of his collar—and he wore old faded jeans that clung nicely to his good parts. He'd even added face paint. "I see you upgraded your fan wear."

Nick nodded and handed the treat to Emily. "Here you go, kid. Have at it." Then he leaned closer and whispered, "Told you I was stepping up my game. Impressed?"

Shelby rolled her eyes as she reached up and tore off the tag, checking the price. "I might have been, but then you went and paid entirely too much for this. I'll send you the link for where I get all my stuff online, dirt cheap."

Nick narrowed his eyes. "Smartass."

Chuckling, she tapped a finger on his warm lips to warn Nick about his language in front of his niece. Shelby glanced down at Emily whose eyes had glazed over as she inhaled her treat. Luckily, Emily was much too interested in her sugar-crack to notice.

When most of it was gone, she glanced up. "Did you want some Shelby?"

"No thanks, sweetheart." Shelby turned to her sexy seatmate who was lost in the game. She poked him in the arm to get his attention. "Why don't you take Emily with you over to the bar so you can share the rest of this treat *together*?"

Nick slowly tore his attention from the field. "I'd rather sit here and share it. You're a lot cuter than those guys."

Yeah, well he was a lot cuter than any guy she'd ever known, and if she weren't careful her hormones were going to ruin her chances with Greg. The guy she'd wanted forever. The right guy. Not Nick, Mr. Love 'Em and Leave 'Em.

Shelby craned her neck behind her to be sure Greg wasn't back. Then she grabbed the front of Nick's jersey and pulled him close. Em was right there, so she whispered in his ear, "Greg'll be back any second and I don't want you here causing trouble. Got it?"

"Trouble? Me?" He grinned. "Don't worry, the prince is out in the hall on the phone. Sounded like something medical and important. He'll probably be a while." He reached up and pulled a wad of pink cotton candy from her hair. "Man this stuff is a mess. Emily, be careful okay? Shelby's trying to look pretty for her date."

Shelby wanted to plop Emily onto his lap and let him deal with the mess, but couldn't hurt Em's feelings. Instead, she leaned so close to Nick she smelled the pine-scented soap on his skin from his shower.

It was strangely erotic.

"Go away. Now!"

"Fine. I can take a hint." He stood and bumped into Greg, spilling the orange soda down his jersey.

"Sorry, Gary. Didn't see you there. Let me go find some napkins."

"It's Greg. Don't bother." His jaw clenched. "I'll be right back, Shelby."

What a freaking disaster.

Shelby stood and pressed Emily, with her sticky hands full of cotton candy, into Nick's arms to go after Greg. "I have to go to the bathroom."

Emily said, "I do too. And Uncle Nick can't take me."

She wanted to scream.

Drawing a deep, calming breath, she shoved the empty cardboard cone at Nick, and then held out her hand to Emily. "Let's go."

They ran into Greg in the hallway outside the bathrooms. His jersey was damp and more orange than usual. At least it blended with the team colors.

She laid a hand on his chest to gauge the wetness of his shirt. "What a mess. I'm sorry."

He laid his hand over hers and gave it a gentle squeeze. "One thing hasn't changed since I left. It's never a dull day when you spend it with Shelby. I'll go grab another drink for Emily and meet you guys back there."

"Thanks." She smiled as they headed for the bathroom. The hand squeeze was a nice touch. But did he think she was high maintenance or something? That'd be bad.

She glanced down at Emily whose little blue eyes, so like Nick's, shined up at her with innocent adoration.

"What do you think he meant by that Monkey-Brains? Never a dull day with me. Is that good or bad?"

"Probably good." Emily grinned. "You're fun, Shelby."

She scooped Em up into her arms and planted a kiss on her forehead. "You're fun too. Even when you're a sticky-icky mess. Let's go get you cleaned up and then see if you can stay that way for a while, huh?"

"Okay." Emily laid her messy hands on either side of Shelby's face and planted a big kiss on her lips. "I love you, Shelby."

Her eyes burned with tears. No one except for Jo had said that to her since her parents had died. "I love you too, Em."

***

Nick grinned as he watched the game. It was the fourth quarter, the Broncos were ahead and Emily was still on Shelby's lap, yakking away. Things were going according to plan. He pulled out his cell and called his sister. When she answered he said, "Call me in five minutes."

Lori snorted. "Hello to you too. Is the plan working?"

"Yup."

"Good. When you get home, I want all the details."

"You got it." Nick tucked his phone into his jeans' back pocket, made his way down to Shelby, and flopped beside her. "Hey. Can I have her back or are you planning a kidnapping?"

The look she sent him as she handed Emily over should have curdled his blood. Instead it just made him even hotter for her.

He feigned innocence. "What?" Before they could get into it, his phone rang. His sister's timing was perfect. He tugged it out of his pocket and stifled his grin. "Hey, Lori."

Pretending to listen, he glanced at Shelby. She was seething. And ignoring Greg who sat on her other side. "Wait. What do you mean you can't pick us up? How are we going to get home?"

Shelby's head whipped toward his and she narrowed her eyes.

He frowned and bit the inside of his cheek to hold back his grin. "But you know after the game we could wait up to an hour for a cab. That'd be rough on Em."

Shelby glared at him now. Steam was going to start rising from her collar any second.

He had to turn away and wrangle the smile that threatened to break his cover. He said to Lori, "Let me ask her if she'd mind." It wasn't easy, but he pulled it together and forced a straight face. "Lori was supposed to pick us up, but she says her car won't start and my mom isn't home. Would you guys mind taking us home?" He hadn't lied. It was what his sister had just said to him.

Shelby gritted her teeth. "You're so lucky Em's here . . ."

"Thanks for the ride."

Shelby was as mad as he'd ever seen her. He'd better tread carefully.

After the game they shuffled along with the crowd out to the parking lot. As they approached Shelby's Prius, the logistics of cramming them all into that clown car ran through his mind. "Shelby, you and Em should sit in the back, and I'll take shotgun." He turned to Greg. "Unless you're letting Shelby drive?"

Before Greg could answer, Shelby shook her head. "Nope, you're just going to have to stuff that big body of yours into the backseat. It'll be fun to watch."

"Shelby, please. Be reasonable. You need to sit in the back."

She grabbed him by the arm and dragged him out of earshot of the others. "I know you don't lie, so your answer will determine your fate. Did you or did you not bring Emily along today to mess with my date with Greg?"

"Are you saying you didn't enjoy Emily's company?"

"No avoidance techniques, answer the question."

Backed firmly into a corner, he huffed out a breath. "Yes."

She nodded sharply. "Change of plans. We'll take Emily to your mother's house and you can think of all the ways you can say you're sorry while you wait for a cab." She stomped away, got into the car, and they left.

Guess he'd found Shelby's limit. Good data point for the future.

He pulled out his phone and ordered a taxi, and then dialed Lori's cell to warn her of the storm approaching named Shelby. When Lori answered, he said, "I can't explain right now, but when Shelby drops Em off, don't let her know what you do for a living. And I need to know how many ways there are to apologize to a woman."

༺ঔ༻

After they'd dropped Emily off, Shelby and Greg headed back to his house. She wasn't sure if Greg was still upset with her or not, so she said, "I'm really sorry about all that. What a mess."

He shrugged. "After my shirt dried things got better."

She laughed, but when she turned to look at him, she saw it wasn't supposed to be funny. That had happened a few times during the game. He seemed different and a lot more serious than he used to be.

Greg definitely didn't have Nick's snappy wit. And he'd been a little quiet all afternoon. Maybe he was still mad about his shirt? "I don't think Nick did that on purpose. I had just told him to get lost right before that, so he was actually following orders."

Staring at the road ahead, Greg said quietly, "He wants you, Shelby. Do you want him?"

In her bed? Yes. But that'd be all she'd ever get, so no. "He doesn't want the same things I do, so it's a moot point as far as I'm concerned."

Greg turned to her and smiled. "What things do you want?"

Would it scare him off if she told the truth? Probably better to lay her cards out. "Eventually, I'd like to be married and have kids. A dog would be good too, but optional."

He chuckled as he pulled up in front of his parents' house. "You'll be a great mom if the way you handled Emily today is any indication. And a great disciplinarian by the way you handled Nick."

She laughed. "He deserved it." And he was so getting that fake set-up date with Jordan as his reward for his bad behavior. Nick knew how much was riding on this date with Greg, so she'd not feel a bit of remorse.

"No argument there." Greg turned the car off and faced her. "This whole thing about not having a car or my own place yet feels like high school." Clearing his throat, he drew a deep breath as if working up to something big.

A kiss maybe?

Greg smiled as he leaned closer and wrapped his arms around her before laying his lips on hers.

About time!

Nice soft mouth, not too dry, not too wet. Good start.

Shelby parted her lips, offering more, and the guy was no fool. He took.

His tongue gently danced with hers, his lips applying just the right pressure. He was a good kisser. What a relief.

But why wasn't that switch that Nick always flipped inside of her doing its thing? She should be quivering with desire, aching for his hands to explore her needy body just as his tongue was doing inside her mouth.

Maybe because she'd waited for this for so long, she was being too analytical? She needed to shut her brain off and just go with it.

Shelby focused on the way his soft tongue tangled with hers, and then she slid a hand behind his neck.

But before she could tug him closer, Greg leaned away, ending their kiss. "They've got me working graveyard so my next night off isn't until Thursday. Want to have dinner? You can pick the place."

Okay. The kiss was a little too short in her estimation, but he'd finally asked her out. Progress at last.

"I'd love to. Something casual?"

He smiled and laid another quick peck on her lips. "Casual's good. I'll call you later to work out the details. Thanks for the game, it was . . . fun."

"Anytime." After Greg got out, Shelby slipped over to the driver's side and then started for home.

Now that was more like it. Things were starting to look up. And he'd finally kissed her.

And the kiss had been . . . okay. It sizzled . . . a little.

Maybe once she relaxed and stopped sweating the details so much, it'd be as hot as any of the kisses Nick had given her. And Greg had finally asked her out. After two long years.

Nice.

So why didn't she feel like singing at the top of her lungs, or least calling Jo to share her good news? It's what she'd wanted for so very long. It could be the start to achieving all she'd hoped for. The first step to the house, handsome husband, two-point-five kids and the pooch she'd always hoped to have.

As she waited for a stoplight to turn, her quick glance in the rearview mirror caught the sight of something pink near her ear. Some of Emily's stray cotton candy.

She plucked out the offending piece of fluff. Glancing at her reflection again, she figured she'd see her victorious smile, not the little frown line splitting the middle of her forehead. Something was off and she couldn't put a label on it. Or maybe she could.

Nick.

Had her anger with Nick spoiled the mood with Greg? No, that wasn't it. She wanted Nick. It was like when a toddler experiences candy for the first time. After savoring something so sweet, nothing else could ever taste as good.

But Nick was like a chocolate truffle. He'd be fantastic at first, then eventually he'd melt away, leaving nothing behind but a fond memory and a few extra pounds of regret to carry around.

Nope. Not going there.

When Shelby walked into her kitchen, Jo sat at the table eating a big bowl of pasta. Shelby hadn't had a chance to talk to Jo outside of the café in days. She missed her best bud.

"Hey stranger. How are you?"

"Good. How was the date?"

"A disaster, but that's Nick's fault." Shelby grabbed a bowl, filled it from the pot on the stove, and joined Jo. Then she told her the whole stupid tale.

"You really made Nick call a cab?"

Shelby stuffed more creamy, garlicy noodles into her mouth and moaned with pleasure. "Damn straight! That was just rude. The man drives me nuts. He's the human version of Chester."

"Yeah, but you couldn't write Chester as well as you do if you weren't a little that way too. Will you promise me something?"

Shelby laid her fork down. Jo's serious tone startled her. "Are you worried about me and you if dating Greg doesn't work out?"

Jo stood and washed her bowl out. When she was done, she turned around and crossed her arms. "No, it's not that. You and I will always be good, no matter what. But you like analogies, so I'm going to give you one. Greg is like your Prius. It's a reliable, steady, and economical vehicle, but it's lacking in flash and speed. Now Nick, he's like your old Porsche. That car was a fast, sexy, powerful ride that didn't make economic sense, but was a hell of a lot of fun to drive. You've made some big changes in your life recently and admit it Shelby, you're still missing your old Porsche."

"Okay, I get your point. But what do you want me to promise?"

"I want you to promise to take your time with Greg. Tell him you just want to be friends until you've become reacquainted again. Don't sleep with him until you're sure he's the same guy you've built him up to be in your mind all these years. You have an honest friendship with him you wouldn't want to ruin. And I don't want to see my brother hurt. But Nick? It'd be torture to always wonder what might have been. I think you should jump his bones as soon as possible so you'll know exactly where you stand with him. Take Nick for a test drive."

A strange sense of relief washed through her. As if Jo saying out loud those same thoughts that Shelby hadn't wanted to face suddenly made them all right. If Emily hadn't been there, would she and Greg have had enough to talk about all afternoon? They were different people now than when they were kids. Maybe she *had* built Greg up in her mind to be more than he could ever be.

"Deal. I'll call Greg tonight and tell him it's strictly platonic for now. I'll even tell him why. He'll probably cancel our dinner date, but you're right, Jo. I need to be fair to your brother."

"Thank you." Jo's lips tilted into one of her trademark smirks. "And Nick?"

She sighed. "I'm so mad at him right now. We'll have to see."

13

"Hanky-panky can lead to big spankies!"
Chester is in Trouble Again

Later the next week, Shelby tapped on her laptop at the café as a big shadow cast over her. Nick. His scrumptious cologne gave him away. Or maybe it was those delectable pheromones of his. "Are you ready to meet your lunch date?"

"I guess. Are you still mad at me?" He sat across from her looking all remorseful, but he wasn't getting off that easy.

"Yep." She slid the Bluetooth that wasn't charged across the table.

He popped it in. "I found something interesting I'd like to show you later if you're free."

"What is it?"

Nick leaned closer and smiled. "You'll have to wait and see, because I think I might have just snagged a huge job. I need to get back to my office as soon as this meet and greet is over. If you weren't already mad at me I would've canceled."

"You'll be glad you didn't cancel. I really think this might be the one for you, Nick. And you know what they say about brunettes. Now go over to that far table and let's do a sound check."

"Okay."

Shelby bit her lip to contain her smile as Nick made his way through the tables filled with diners. When he sat down and grinned at her, she struggled for a stern look.

Payback time.

She pretended to speak so Nick could see her mouth move. He tapped at his earpiece. Frowning, he took it out and examined it.

Finally he lifted it up and mouthed, "Not working."

She stood and crossed to his table. She pretended to mess with it a bit and then said, "Shoot. Your date will be here any minute. I guess you're on your own this time. Sorry."

Nick shook his head. "You know what? Maybe it'd be best to cancel since I really don't have time for this anyway."

"Are you scared to do it alone?"

"No, of course not." He huffed out a breath and glanced at his heavy gold watch. "But if she's late I'm not waiting more than ten minutes for her."

She patted his shoulder. "Okay. I need to talk to Jo about something. Remember your manners and make good choices."

Nick scowled at her. "Make good choices? What are you talking about?"

"You'll see. Bye."

Shelby quickly disappeared into the kitchen. On the far wall in the back, two big flat-screens showed all the angles from their security cams, both inside and outside the café. Shelby grabbed a stool and waited for the show to begin.

Jo, wiping her hands on a towel, stood nearby. "Too bad we don't have sound. That would've made this so much better."

Jordan showed up, head swiveling looking for Nick. She'd given Jordan a description of Nick, so it didn't take long before the very handsome Jordan headed Nick's way and introduced himself. Jordan could model for GQ and had the best sense of humor of any of her friends.

The look on Nick's face when he'd realized Jordan was his date—priceless. "See the way his jaw is slightly clenching, Jo? He's livid."

Jo's chuckle was downright evil. "A vein in his forehead is popping. He's definitely going to kill you. Or have a stroke."

"Well, wait. It gets better." Shelby turned her attention back to the screen. When Jordan reached out and laid a hand on Nick's arm, Nick's eyes shifted, as if looking for the fastest escape route.

Nick, clearly uncomfortable, stood to leave. Jordan laughed, held up a hand to stop him, and must have confessed it was a joke, just as Act Two came strolling in. A tall, beautiful blonde client who was also an actress who Shelby'd recruited to play a role in her payback plan.

Throwing an elbow into Jordan's ribs in a "get lost" gesture, the blonde smiled sweetly at Nick.

Relief crossed Nick's face as he shook her hand and pulled out a chair for her.

Jo said, "She's gorgeous, Shelby. Aren't you afraid he might go for her instead of you?"

"No. She's perfect on the *outside* just like Nick originally ordered." Shelby's lips tilted in anticipation. "But you can't always judge a book by its cover. If she doesn't make him blow a gasket, nothing will."

"You're a brave woman." Jo patted her shoulder. "But you may have to hide out for a few days."

While Nick and the actress talked, Shelby checked e-mails on her phone. After answering a few, she looked up again. Nick's table was empty.

That was fast.

Both the kitchen's double doors banged open. "Dammit, Shelby! Where are you?"

Whoops.

The fury in Nick's voice had her making a run for it. If she could get to Jo's office before him, maybe she could lock the door until he calmed down.

She sped down the short hallway stacked with baking supplies on either side, his loud footsteps warning her he was close.

When she reached the office, she slapped the door closed behind her, but a loud thud, followed by Nick's vicious curse, told her he'd taken it in the face.

So not good!

Shelby rounded the desk and stood behind it, grateful for the solid piece of furniture that would separate her from the madman.

Nick threw the door open and stalked inside with a big red mark on his forehead and murderous intent in his eyes.

"I didn't mean to hit you with the door, Nick. Sorry."

"You were smart to run." He started toward her, but she slipped around the side. He feinted left, then went right, but Shelby was a decent basketball player and didn't fall for it.

"Give it up Shelby, you can't escape."

"We'll see about that." She made a big move that left him on the backside of the desk and her on the front, closer to the door. "Bye!"

156

She ran full tilt into the hall, smiling at the prospect of escape through the swinging doors. Her forward progress came to an abrupt halt when Nick wrapped his tree trunk of an arm around her waist. Then her feet left the ground, and he threw her over his shoulder, knocking the air out of her lungs.

"The day a little runt like you outmaneuvers me is the day I'm washed up."

Shelby hung upside down, struggling for air, staring at Nick's fine rear end. "My heels slowed me down, but admit it. I outmaneuvered you, pal."

"You play dirty. First a guy, then her? She laughed like a . . . braying donkey. I've never heard anything so obnoxious."

"Some might call her laugh a unique trait."

"Or, some might call it payback times ten."

Yep. She'd asked the actress to be over the top obnoxious and it apparently worked. But since she was in no position to gloat at the moment, she kept her mouth shut and admired his butt.

He carried her back to the office and kicked the door closed behind them. His large hand lightly smacked her bottom before he righted her, then dropped her to her feet. What little breath she had slipped out of her lungs as Nick used his whole body to press her back against the wall.

He was damn sexy when he was mad.

Nick trapped her hands above her head with one of his, and pressed his body even closer. She should probably try to start breathing again.

"Now who's outmaneuvered, Shelby? Say you're sorry, and mean it, and I might let you off with just a kiss." The raw lust in his gaze dampened her panties. She forgot all about her screaming lungs.

"Nope. What else you got?" She couldn't help it, her lips tilted into a grin that was sure to piss him off even more. There was no one more fun to fight with than Nick.

He leaned down and whispered, "I might have to kiss you all over until you give in."

Her heart leapt. "I'm pretty stubborn."

"I know." All his anger seemed to recede as his mouth formed a slow, sexy smile before starting his assault along the hollow at the base of her neck. She tilted her chin and moaned as his lips slowly traveled up to her earlobe and gave it a gentle bite.

He whispered, "Give in yet?"

She shook her head. "Not even close. Maybe it'd help if you let go of my hands?" She wanted to touch him so badly she ached for it.

"Nope. You'll probably knock me over the head with something." With his free hand, he unfastened the top two buttons of her blouse, and his mouth ventured south.

She shivered in delight.

"Are you sorry now?" he asked with his face buried in her chest.

"Not a bit." She laid a soft kiss on the mark on his forehead. "Maybe you should kiss me like you did the other day. That was pretty annoying."

He chuckled. "I want you, Shelby."

Her heart pounded, sending even more heat downstairs. "Jo thinks I'll always wonder if I don't sleep with you."

His head lifted and then he nipped her bottom lip. "I like Jo."

Shelby sucked his full bottom lip into her mouth and nipped him back. "So do I. But I'm still mad at you. You don't deserve it."

Instead of arguing, he kissed her just like she'd asked him to. Slow, sweet, and deep.

Lust danced a jive within her belly again.

Jo's voice interrupted their fun. "Good job, Nick. I bet Shelby's learned her lesson good and proper now. But do you guys mind? I have work to do."

His lips curved against Sheby's as he released her hands, quickly buttoned her blouse, and took a step back. "I have to get back to work. Can I come over for dinner tonight and show you what I found? And then maybe we could discuss Jo's theory some more."

"Sure. But which theory? The one about brunettes being better in bed? Did you decide to sleep with Jordan after all?"

His eyes narrowed. "I'll be there at seven, wiseass." He gave her butt a pat. "I'll bring a pizza." He smirked as he strutted out the door.

Shelby called out to his big back, "You need to wipe that self-assured look off of your face, pal. We still have a lot of terms to discuss. It's not a given that I'm going to sleep with you."

Jo rolled her eyes and slipped behind her desk. "Really, Shelby?"

Okay, it was a given.

Shelby made her way out to her car and smiled all the way home.

After her long bubble bath, she donned her black push up bra and put on the new sexy low-cut blouse she'd just bought. For once in her life, she wanted to be the bad girl instead of the good one. Maybe she'd punished herself enough for her deeds as a child.

It was Nick's struggles with his own issues that made her see her own behavior more clearly. Guilt controlled his life like she'd let her childhood mistake control hers.

Nick was just the one to unlock her bad girl's bedroom door and let her out to play. She could be that woman who just wanted great sex, nothing more. Or at least she was going to try.

When she'd called Greg after her talk with Jo to explain how she wanted to keep things platonic between them, he'd said he totally agreed. She needed to see what was between her and Nick. Greg didn't want to be with a woman who'd wonder what she'd missed. That was just so . . . Greg-like of him. Most guys would have told her to take a flying leap. But not sensible, reliable Greg the Prius. And he still wanted to have dinner, just as friends, because he'd missed her.

Perfect situation. Happiness all around.

When the doorbell rang at seven on the dot, her heart nearly stopped. She drew a deep breath, channeled her best bad girl, and told herself one more time that it was okay to have a fun fling.

She opened the door and there he was with a big smile, his briefcase, and a large pizza box.

"Hi, Pizza Boy. Come inside and we'll figure out a way for you to earn a big tip."

Maybe she should tone it down a bit. She didn't want to appear *that* easy. Better to make him work for it. At least a little.

Nick grinned as he slipped past her. "I did this in college to earn extra money. You're talking to a man who knows how to maximize his tips."

"Really?" Shelby shut the door behind him. "You delivered pizzas?"

He crossed over to the kitchen and laid the box on the counter. "I did."

"So, did you ever swap naughty acts for tips?"

Nick pulled her against him. "Define naughty." He kissed her but she couldn't concentrate, because she experienced a sudden overwhelming wave of writer's curiosity and needed to know the truth. She leaned back and ended their kiss. "Seriously. Did you?"

"No. I kept it professional. Strictly dollar bills. But I have something I want to show you. Promise you won't get mad at me for doing this without asking first."

Warning bells went off. Shelby took a step back, wrapping her arms around her waist. "Okay . . . what?"

Nick led her to a chair in the kitchen and laid a file in front of her. "This is the report from the night of your fire."

As he flipped a few pages, bile rose in Shelby's throat. Slow burning rage seared the lining of her stomach. And to think she'd actually thought they'd become friends. Good friends.

"Why would you do this to me?"

When she started to rise from her chair, Nick's strong arms held her in place. "Read it, Shelby. Please?"

"Dammit, Nick, no! Let me go." Those muscles she once thought were sexy now held her prisoner. No matter how hard she struggled, his firm grip never faltered.

Anger, fear, and Nick's betrayal conjured tears that all her efforts couldn't stop from running down her cheeks. When a soft sob escaped her throat, Nick laid a gentle kiss on her cheek.

He whispered, "I'd never hurt you, Shelby. Please?" He pointed to a yellow highlighted sentence. "Right here."

The truth in his voice seeped inside her chest and wrapped itself around her heart, giving it a warm hug. No, Nick wouldn't be intentionally cruel. It was the fire and her mistake she didn't want to face.

Her vision swam as she tried to focus. She blinked away her tears and suddenly the line became clear. *The fire originated in the master bedroom in an ashtray by the bed.*

She couldn't breathe. It was like when Nick threw her over his shoulder but ten times worse. She opened her mouth to suck in air and finally was able to whisper, "I didn't kill them?"

"No. It wasn't your fault. Your parents must've been partying like you said they often did. You did everything you could to save your sister, but it was your parents who killed her. Not you, Shelby. They found traces of drugs. It looks like your uncle paid someone to ensure this report stayed buried deep enough that the media wouldn't taint your family's name."

"Thank you, Nick." Shelby crossed her arms on the tabletop in front of her and laid her head down. All her years of guilt and frustration rose up like a tidal wave through her body, begging for release. She cried so hard, she could barely catch her breath between the sobs.

Nick stuck a paper towel in her hand, scooped her up, and then sat down in the chair and placed her on his lap, wrapping her up in his big arms. He tucked her head under his chin as the waterworks flowed.

It must've been fifteen minutes of bawling on him before she sat up, realizing she was absolutely free of guilt for the first time in twenty-two years. It felt fantastic and she wanted to celebrate. And after that, she'd kill her aunt and uncle for never telling her the truth. How could they have been so heartless? But then, she'd never told them how she felt about losing her family, and they'd never asked.

As she blew her nose on the scratchy paper towel, something occurred to her. She tilted her head up and stared into Nick's pretty blue eyes. "If my uncle had the report buried, how did you get it?"

He swallowed hard. "My dad. When things didn't add up, he called in a few favors from some powerful friends."

Her eyes grew misty all over again. *She* was the friend Nick had done the favor for by asking his dad for help? If she wasn't careful she was going to fall so hard, there'd be no return from Mr. One-Night Stand land.

Nope. She needed to take what she planned to share with him at face value. Just sex, nothing more. No more Miss Goody Two–Shoes and no more obsessive worries about what happened next. It was oddly freeing.

"I know how hard that was to ask your dad, so I'm calling in that rain check. You're getting lucky for your good deed. Let's go." She hopped off his lap and tugged on his hand.

Nick grinned, but didn't budge. "That's not why I did it, Shelby. So you'd sleep with me." He slipped his hand from hers, then stood and wrapped her up in his arms. "You have a lot to process. I'd better go." He laid a soft kiss on her forehead.

God he was sweet.

"No, you don't understand, Nick. I've decided to try it your way. I *want* to expand my horizons and try a fun one-night stand. And I want it with you."

His smile slowly bloomed. "You want to sleep with me?"

"Yes. I've got big plans for that body of yours. Let's go."

He stood in place as a frown canceled out his earlier sexy grin. "Wait. What if—"

She cut him off with a kiss. She was totally ready to have mindless, hot, no-strings-attached sex.

Probably.

14

> "Chester loved speed. Slapping his skateboard down at the top of a hill he'd never tried before, he jumped on, and then went faster than he ever had. It was fun trying something new."
> *Chester Gets a New Skateboard*

Shelby tugged Nick into her bedroom and closed the door. Then she backed him up against it and kissed him as she slipped his suit coat off his shoulders. She quickly unknotted his tie and threw it over her shoulder.

His hands wandered over her body, heating everywhere he touched as he tried to take charge, but she grabbed his wrists and held them tight. "Nope. It's my victory party and you'll just have to grin and bear it. I'm going to do all the things I've wanted to do to you since I saw the photos of those big muscles of yours on Facebook. You were right, they drive women crazy."

"And yet you made me get rid of them." He laughed and then gave her a hard kiss.

"I was doing my job." As she unbuttoned his white, starched shirt, she laid kisses on the newly exposed skin, his low moans spurring her on. He had a fantastic body. Those pictures hadn't done him justice. Her lips couldn't help but linger and explore all the peaks and valleys of his beautiful chest.

Forcing herself to stay on track and get to the good stuff, she unbuckled Nick's belt and threw it aside. Then she lowered his zipper. "And maybe I didn't like the idea of those women sending you naked pictures."

"I wouldn't mind if you sent me some, but keep that up and this party's going to end in about three seconds. It's been awhile." He leaned down and kissed her. "We're doing this my way. The first time. After that, you can do anything to me your heart desires. Unless it involves that bat of yours."

Before she could protest, he scooped her up and carried her to the bed.

Nick had them both stripped naked, with her under him, in less than thirty seconds. "I'm going to start with your toes and work my way up."

Hot panic rushed through her at the thought of Nick's mouth on her legs. It was one thing to get naked with him, but entirely another for him to actually focus on her damaged skin. Why couldn't he be like the other guys she'd slept with who just sort of ignored her legs?

"I . . . won't . . . be able to feel much. Why don't you start at the top?"

"Nope." He kissed her deeply before he whispered, "Relax and enjoy."

Relax? That was the last thing she'd be able to do. When he slid to the bottom of the bed she squeezed her eyes shut. She didn't want to see the look on his face when he got the up close and personal view of her skin. Why hadn't she thought to kill the lights? Probably because she wanted to see him as much as he apparently wanted to see her. He'd change his mind about that soon enough.

When he'd seen her legs before, he'd said he wasn't repulsed by them, but what if he was just being nice? Maybe sleeping with Nick had been a big mistake.

As he lifted her foot to his mouth, she fisted her hands in the sheets and prayed it'd be over quickly so they could just get to the good part.

Odd little licks of thrill running up her spine forced her eyes open in surprise. Nick sent her a knowing grin and then went back to work.

No one had ever kissed her toes before, she had no idea. Closing her eyes again, she drew a deep breath, released her death grip on the sheets, and tried to focus on the slight, sensual sparks that came and went. Who knew toe-kissing could be so sexy?

Then his hands and mouth moved higher, up to her calves, slowly caressing them with his long fingers and soft lips. When his tongue found the back of her knee, a zap of heat shot through her so hard and fast she jerked in surprise.

If Nick could do this to her by just touching her mostly numb legs, what was it going to be like when he got to the top of them? She couldn't wait to find out.

But the warm buzz waned a bit as her worries crept back again about what he must be thinking about her marred skin. She pried her eyes open and blinked in surprise at the lust in Nick's gaze as he softly kissed her knee.

He seemed to be enjoying this as much as she was.

Maybe her legs weren't as bad to look at as she'd always thought.

She closed her eyes again, determined to enjoy the ride.

He finally moved high enough that she felt his warm breath heat her inner thighs. Just a little higher and he'd be able to focus on the undamaged parts of her and they'd be all good. Maybe then she could draw a deep breath again.

With each inch he advanced, she could feel more and more of his soft caresses. A warm wave of pleasure built deep inside, spreading gently throughout her whole body. Nick moved so slow it drove her insane, but if he stopped she'd kill him.

And then as if reading her mind, he stopped. "Look at me, Shelby."

Really? Now?

She cracked one eye open. "What?"

"Both eyes. I want to tell you something."

She huffed out a breath and opened the other eye. Why did she ever agree to let him be in charge? "You're killing me here, Nick."

He slid up her body and lifted her face between his rough palms. Then he kissed her lips so gently it just wasn't fair. Her annoyance with him instantly disappeared.

After he'd made her mind go all mushy, he leaned back and beamed that sexy you-know-you-want-me grin of his. And she did. More than she'd ever wanted anyone else before. Or probably would ever again, so he needed to hurry up with whatever he wanted to say and get back to it.

"You're an incredibly beautiful woman, Shelby."

"This is a one-night stand, remember? You don't have to say stuff like that. I know I'm not—"

"Stop." He growled before he dipped his head down and then used those capable lips on her neck, then her shoulders, then back to her mouth again.

She stared into his eyes, so filled with emotion she'd be a fool to argue they spoke anything other than the truth, and her heart soared. Nick was the only man who had ever made her feel pretty despite her ugly legs.

A sigh escaped as something shifted uncomfortably in her chest. He really and truly thought she was beautiful. If they never slept together again that'd be okay, because just him saying it, meaning it, would be something she'd always treasure. When happy tears threatened to escape, she figured maybe she'd better lighten things up a bit. This was a one-night stand. Nothing more. And there was no crying during sex. Or was that baseball?

Didn't matter.

Then he kissed her so deeply her mind couldn't focus on anything else. She could happily kiss Nick for hours.

When his full lips left hers, she drew a deep breath and let go of all the tension she'd bottled up as his mouth slowly left hot trails of pleasure down her body again. Just when she didn't think she could stand another second of his glorious torture, he made his way even further south. For a man in a hurry, he was making sure she was insane with need before he got his due. Big points there.

He laid slow kisses on her stomach and then her inner thighs, finally hitting the bull's-eye. Her back arched in silent invitation.

Nick obviously got the hint, because he smiled and said, "My turn."

He wrapped her up tight in his arms and whispered, "You're perfect Shelby," and her heart was forever his.

But it was the way he stared so deeply into her eyes as he moved inside her and made love to her that sent an overwhelming need to kiss him, to share the rapture raging through her with him. She ran her hand into his thick hair and pulled his head down to hers again. The powerful need in their kiss accelerated her trip to the edge of the cliff she so badly needed to jump off of. Unable to stand another second, she pleaded, "Now, Nick. Please?"

And they both dove off the cliff together.

As her heart rate settled a bit, Shelby ran her fingernails up and down Nick's damp back. He weighed a ton, but in a nice way. She laid a soft kiss on his cheek. "I can't imagine how Beth put up with *that* for two whole years."

He laughed and nipped her shoulder. "It wasn't like that with her, Shelby. Or anyone else."

"Does that mean it was really good for you too? Because—"

"It was fantastic. Now what about that pizza?"

Typical man, worried about his stomach at a time like this. "I'll go warm it up." She poked him in the ribs. "Move it."

After he switched their positions so she was on top, she started to roll off of him, but he stopped her and pulled her close. He stared into her eyes again before he kissed her. It was slow, sweet, sensuous, and somehow different than any of the other times he'd kissed her before. "Thank you, Shelby."

She wasn't sure if he was thanking her for the sex or for getting the pizza. Unfamiliar with after-a-one-night-stand etiquette she simply replied, "You're welcome," then quickly found her robe and padded to the kitchen. She put three slices of pizza in the toaster oven and then grabbed two bottles of beer from the fridge. While she waited for the pizza to heat, she leaned against the counter and closed her eyes.

She'd never felt that before. It was like she could feel his pleasure as if it were her own. And the way he'd just kissed her? The heat still lingered on her lips. Had she gone and ruined everything by falling in love with a man who wasn't capable of loving her back?

By the time the toaster oven dinged, she figured Nick would have joined her in the kitchen in his rush to get out the door and maintain his never-spending-the-night policy. But because he hadn't, she loaded everything on a tray and headed back to her bedroom.

Nick, still naked except for the sheet tossed carelessly over his waist, was on her side of the bed, digging through her nightstand drawer. Paying her back for the other night, no doubt.

Watching him made her whole body heat again at the memory of what they'd just shared. "Looking for something in particular?"

"No, just snooping." He held up a paperback book. "Any good?"

She laid the tray on her nightstand, thrilled he was still there and that things weren't awkward. "Fantastic, and I'm done so you can have it. Move over. You're on my side of the bed."

"This is my side too. I can't sleep on the other side."

She sat on the edge of the bed and handed him a slice of pizza. "I thought you'd be dressed and ready to bolt out the door by now."

He shook his head before taking a huge bite. "Nope. I'm not done with you yet. I figured we'd eat and then I'd let you have your way with me. And in the morning, I'll make you breakfast. I make awesome eggs."

Shelby's heart did a backflip. If she'd been wearing panties, they'd have melted right off.

And he was even going to cook? "Okay. But we're going to have to talk about who's sleeping on this side of the bed."

Nick reached for his beer and took a long pull. "We'll share."

"We'll see." She took another bite and smiled at how pretty his face was, except for his one little flaw. "How'd you break your nose?"

His pizza stopped halfway to his lips. "It's embarrassing."

She finished off her pizza, took a slug from her beer and then straddled him. "Maybe I'll just have to kiss you all over until you crack."

He tossed what was left of his second slice onto the tray. "I'm pretty stubborn."

"I know." Shelby slipped off her robe and ran kisses over his hard chest. "But I'm relentless."

Nick closed his eyes and groaned. "Thank God."

After a few minutes of kisses and torture she said, "Tell."

"Dammit, Shelby," he growled.

"Okay. Fine. You know what? I'm bored."

She started to roll off of him, but his big hands stopped her and then he flipped her onto her back. "Bored? You're gonna pay for that."

She could hardly wait for whatever punishment he had in mind. Just as he was about to show her, she placed a hand on his chest. "Nope, not unless you tell."

A vein swelled on his forehead as he narrowed his eyes. "Lori hit a line drive that took a bad bounce."

"Your sister broke your nose with a baseball?" She laughed so hard her ribs hurt. "I love that."

Nick ignored her laughter, more concerned with their unfinished business. He kissed the sensitive skin in front of her ear, sending a delicious shiver up her spine, and whispered, "It was a *bad* bounce. Focus, Shelby."

She closed her eyes as a smile lingered on her lips. "'Kay."

Nick ran his hand through his still-damp hair as he monitored the bacon bubbling in the pan on the stove. What had he been thinking? He'd just broken all his own damned rules. He'd planned to show her the fire report, eat some pizza, and then be on his way. He had an important proposal to finish.

But instead he'd spent the night. And what a night. But what if she found out what he'd been up to? It'd hurt her even worse. That's the last thing he wanted to do.

But Shelby wanted to be with *him*, too. The desire in her eyes made her impossible to resist.

And then he'd gone and done the one thing he swore he'd never do. Fall in love. But if he were honest, his plan had fallen apart shortly after he'd met her. Shelby was like no one else. And to think, he worried it'd be Shelby who'd get too attached if they slept together. Looks like the joke was on him.

His plan to shred the report he'd originally planned to give to his sister and never tell Shelby about it wasn't going to work. The guilt, and weirdly, his grandmother's voice in his head, told him it would just eat at him. He needed to come clean. Would she understand if he told her about his grandmother? And explain he hadn't stolen files or computer lists, nothing illegal. That he'd stopped spying and snooping right when he realized he had feelings for her. And that he hadn't and wouldn't give the information he'd learned to Lori.

Then he'd find some other way to keep his promise to his grandmother and save her matchmaking legacy.

Shaking off the negative thoughts, he plucked the bacon out and laid it on a paper towel to drain. Then he cracked eggs into the bacon grease the way his mom always did.

But his mind kept shifting back to Shelby. Was he what was best for her? No one in his family had ever stayed married.

Hell, his mom hadn't even remarried in the past twenty years. It wasn't in their genes, apparently.

Shelby'd told him Greg's parents had been together for almost forty years. That's the kind of background a guy should have to be good enough for Shelby. Greg would instinctively know what he had to do to make a family and a marriage work. Nick had no clue.

What had he gone and done?

"Something smells fantastic." Shelby slipped her arms around his waist and kissed his bare back. "Not that I don't like the view, but cooking bacon shirtless could get painful if you're not careful."

When he turned and kissed her, his doubts disappeared. No one but him deserved to kiss Shelby every morning like this. Greg could find his own woman.

He reluctantly broke their kiss. "I couldn't find my shirt. But good timing, everything's almost ready."

Convinced he could pull off his new plan, he dished up their breakfast. Meanwhile, Shelby poured the coffee and snagged the bread from the toaster. It was nice, working together. Not awkward at all to be with her after they'd made love most of the night.

After they sat, Shelby handed him a napkin and smiled. "He's good in bed and cooks too? Best one-night stand ever."

He held her gaze. "That wasn't a one-night stand, Shelby. I'll be busy with a client who's flying in for the weekend, so will you have dinner with me tonight?"

"Sure." Her eyes lit up as she nibbled on a piece of bacon. "Maybe we should stay in and finish off that pizza?"

"Sounds like a plan."

He'd find a way to tell her the truth so she'd understand. Problem solved.

15

> "Chester needed a foolproof plan to convince Julie to go to the dance with him."
> ***Chester is in Love***

Nick leaned back in his leather chair at work, propped his loafers onto his desk, and bounced a Styrofoam basketball off the ceiling. He needed a come-clean plan.

Maybe on Monday, after he signed the deal with his new client he could celebrate with Shelby. He'd take her to that great Italian place where he'd met the crazy crystal lady. Shelby said the lasagna was her favorite.

Over dessert, he'd tell her he loved her, and then . . . what? Ease into it by explaining about his grandmother? How Grams had tears in her eyes when she'd begged him to save Lori's business? For Emily's sake. Explain he hadn't wanted to hurt her, and then reinforce how last night had been the best night of his life?

No, that wouldn't work. It made her seem less important than his family. She'd probably tell him he was a jerk and dump her tiramisu over his head.

Shelby'd do it, too.

He chuckled as he caught the spongy ball bouncing back toward his face.

No, he should tell her he loved her right up front—but that he'd made a Chester-like mistake and promise nothing like it would ever happen again. Then he'd tell her what he'd done. Which really wasn't anything because he hadn't given the report to his sister, but Shelby wouldn't see it that way once she found out Lori was a matchmaker too.

Then he'd grovel if necessary.

Yeah. That might work. And to keep his promise to Grams, he'd come clean with Lori and convince her she needed to accept his help to bring her business into the twenty-first century. Lori had excellent instincts when it came to matching people up, just like his grandmother had. Lori just needed to expand her business and networking skills.

Done and done.

Swinging his feet to the floor, he waggled his mouse and searched for the restaurant to make a reservation for Monday night. The sooner he got the truth out the better.

A loud beep interrupted his date-planning. "Mr. Caldwell? Mr. Duncan's assistant is on the line. He wonders what time the dinner reservation is for tomorrow night?"

"Seven. And would you call Beth Gunderson and ask if she can join us? Our new client is looking for legal counsel too."

"Will do."

If Beth weren't the best in her field he'd have found someone else. But he wanted to nail down the deal. It was a big contract. It'd bring in a ton of new work if he could handle the buy-out Duncan had in mind. It'd be a tough challenge, but one he was up for. Failure was not an option. Could be the most important weekend of his career.

After he'd made the dinner reservation for Monday with Shelby, he closed the restaurant page and got back to work. If he could get the final touches on the proposal done before lunch, he'd go eat with Shelby at the café.

Just the thought of sharing a meal with Shelby made him smile. Man he had it bad for her.

~

Shelby hadn't stopped grinning since Nick left earlier. And she couldn't wait to spread her happy news. Slapping the café kitchen doors open, she found her target. Jo stood at a steel countertop with her hands buried deep in bread dough.

Waving the papers Nick brought the night before in front of Jo's face, she said, "I'm finally guilt-free."

"What are you talking about?" Jo sprinkled flour on the tabletop.

"My family. The fire. It wasn't me. See?" Shelby held the paper steady and pointed.

Jo punched her floury dough out on her table as she leaned down to read the highlighted sentence. Tilting her head as she took it in, Jo suddenly threw her messy hands around Shelby and pulled her into a tight hug. "Oh, Shelby. That's the best news ever. You must be so relieved." Jo held on and rocked them back and forth as she sniffed back her tears. Jo understood the huge impact that the one sentence carried. She was the best friend a girl could ever have.

Shelby nodded against Jo's shoulder. "It's like I lost the twenty pounds of regret I've made myself haul around all these years."

Jo leaned back and smiled. "And I noticed a fancy sports car parked in front of the house this morning when I left. I thought he never spends the night. What did you do? Handcuff him to the bed?"

"No, but handcuffs might be fun." Shelby laughed as she swiped flour and bits of dough off her blouse. "He just declared he was staying. He even made breakfast this morning. We're having dinner tonight."

"Wow. Maybe you're the one who'll change his ways. So . . . how was it? The sleeping together part."

"It was amazing. Different than with anyone else. Off-the-charts good. And he cuddles too." Shelby laid a hand over her swelling heart. "I think I'm in love with him, Jo."

Jo wrapped Shelby up in a hug again and whispered, "I'm so happy for you. Why don't you go sit down and I'll cut into the Death by Chocolate cake I just made. Then you can fill me in on all the deets."

"Beth will be here in a few minutes for her date. But she doesn't need me other than to make the introductions. I'll go grab some tables."

Still smiling and not sure her feet were actually touching the ground she was so freaking happy, she found a table for Beth and her date, and then one nearby for her and Jo.

Just as she'd settled in, her phone signaled a text. Beth's date was going to have to cancel. It would have been nice if he'd figured that out sooner than five minutes before he was supposed to show. She quickly tapped out a note to Beth, doubting she'd catch her before she left her office.

When the front doors parted, she glanced up, expecting to see Beth. But Nick's sister Lori entered instead. Shelby saw her scan the café until their eyes locked on each other's. Lori smiled that same big smile as Nick's.

Waving her over, she said, "Hi, Lori. Want to join me?"

177

"Thank you." Lori hung her purse on the back of the chair and sat. "Nick mentioned you often write here, so I'd hoped I'd run into you. I wanted to ask you a favor."

"Sure. What?"

"It's Emily's birthday on Saturday. Nick, the knucklehead, told her he'd pay for any party she wanted because he has a this-guy-can-take-my-business-into-the-next-stratosphere client in town last minute and won't be able to come. So of course she picked the place I had already nixed."

"I'll bet Emily is disappointed."

"She is. My brother can be so . . ." Lori huffed out a breath. "Anyway, Emily asked if she could invite you, and then introduce you to her friends. They all want to meet the lady who writes Chester books. But I don't want you to feel obligated. I can tell her you have other plans if you'd rather not come."

"I'd love to come. And I'll bring books to sign for Emily's friends." If things worked out with Nick, Emily might be her niece one day too. The thought warmed her already ridiculously blissful heart. But then a sliver of disappointment with Nick crept in. "You'd think Nick could slip away for an hour or so. It is Saturday, after all." Maybe she'd mention the idea to him later over dinner. It'd mean a lot to Emily.

"You'd think." Lori shook her head. "Nick works too much. It's been nice to see him relax a little and have fun with you these last few weeks, Shelby."

Just as she opened her mouth to reply, a clearly pissed-off Beth marched up to their table. "I got your text in the parking lot, Shelby. Scratch that guy off the list. I don't have time for inconsiderate people." Then she turned to Lori. "Hi. How've you been?"

"Good." Lori smiled. "I didn't realize you knew Shelby."

Beth nodded as she yanked out a chair and plopped onto it. Probably her skyscraper heels were paining her. "She's setting me and Nick up on dates. I was a little surprised when Nick chose Shelby for our matchmaker instead of you."

Lori's head whipped in Shelby's direction. "Matchmaker? But you write Chester books."

"I do both." Confused, Shelby asked, "You're a matchmaker too?" Then it dawned on her. "Are you Lori Went? As in the radio ads that say, 'I went with Lori and found my soul mate,' Lori Went?"

Lori's brow crumpled as she nodded. "But why would Nick use you instead of me?"

Beth said, "Maybe he's spying on his sister's biggest competitor? He *is* in the business of improving businesses, after all."

Lori shook her head. "No, he wouldn't . . ." She cut herself off and her eyes widened as if she'd thought of a reason. "I'm sure there's a good explanation for this, Shelby."

Beth's lips tilted into a smug grin. "Well it might explain why Nick stopped sleeping with me. He was too busy pretending to be interested in his sister's competitor. I'll bet he'll be knocking on my door tonight now, instead of waiting for our date tomorrow night." Beth sent Shelby a take-that-loser eyebrow hitch.

"Date tomorrow night? That can't be . . ." Nick said he had a client in town.

Shelby's delusional heart broke into a million pieces.

She *was* a loser.

"He called this morning." Beth pulled out her phone and scrolled through the call list. She flipped it around. "See?"

A call from Caldwell and Associates.

Proof.

A few hours earlier, Nick had said what they'd shared wasn't a one-night stand. She'd been an idiot to think he'd changed. That he wanted to have a real relationship. He'd just been using her. To help his sister.

Beth rolled her eyes. "What? Did you really think you were the *one* who could change a guy like Nick? He's never going to be the settle-down-and-have-a-family type, Shelby." Beth stood and swept her hands down her sides. "If this body couldn't do it, a little pixie like you doesn't stand a chance, honey."

With a mean chuckle, Beth turned and left.

When Shelby met Lori's gaze, pity reflected back. Yeah. Pity for the loser with the scarred legs who was dumb enough to believe anyone as perfect as Nick could ever want to have a serious relationship with *her*. Beth was right.

Warm tears spilled down her cheeks. She clenched her teeth to stop her chin from trembling. She was embarrassing herself even more in front of Nick's sister.

She stood to leave.

Lori reached out and grabbed Shelby's hand. "I didn't know anything about this, I swear, Shelby."

Lori's mouth continued to move, but Shelby couldn't hear the words with all the blood pounding so loudly in her ears.

There just wasn't enough air to breathe. She had to go.

Tugging her hand free of Lori's grip, Shelby headed for the door. Jo called out from behind, but Shelby didn't stop. She couldn't, she'd fall completely apart.

She cursed Nick Caldwell for making a fool out of her.

❦

Nick crossed the parking lot and headed for the café. Beth's BMW zipped past him, nearly taking off his toes. Must be late for something.

He hadn't heard back from his assistant about whether Beth was joining him for Duncan's dinner. He'd have to ask when he got back.

Tugging the café's door open, he spotted Shelby headed his way. Behind her, Jo and Lori called out for Shelby to wait, but she didn't stop. What the heck was wrong?

When Shelby glanced up, he froze. Her cheeks were as pale as they were on the day at the hospital when she'd almost fainted. Tears flowed down her face.

When their eyes met, Shelby's eyes went stone cold.

His heart sank.

Beth was just here and so was Lori.

Shelby knew about the spying. The anger in Lori's eyes confirmed it. He called out, "Shelby, I—"

She held up a hand to cut him off as she slipped past him and out the front door.

Shelby had just beeped the locks open on her car when he caught up with her. He slipped a hand around her arm to slow her down. "Please stop, Shelby. I can explain."

She jerked her elbow from his grasp. "Don't touch me."

He took a step back. "Sorry. I just—"

"How could you lie to me like that?" Her chin quivered as she wiped away her tears with both hands. "And then sleep with me on top of it!"

Lori and Jo caught up and stood nearby, as if ready to jump to Shelby's aid.

"Technically, I never lied to you, Shelby." When she closed her eyes and shook her head, he immediately wished he could take his words back. His mind scrambled for the right ones. "What I should have said, was—"

"Don't bother, Nick. I had myself fooled into thinking you'd changed. That you were the right guy for me. Ready to give a real relationship a try. Instead it had all been a lie. You're no different than your father. A liar and a cheat."

Her words hit him like a hard slap across the face. "No, Shelby . . ."

"Tell me the truth, Nick. Have you been spying on my business?" Her eyes narrowed with anger again.

He slowly nodded. "Yes, but it was for my—"

She cut him off. "And *do* you have a dinner date with Beth tomorrow night?"

"Yes, but it's a business dinner, Shelby." She was slipping away from him, dammit. He couldn't lose her. "My client needed a lawyer like Beth. I swear. Nothing more."

She blinked for a second, as if processing, then plowed on. "Regardless. That you'd still do business with Beth after you broke up, when she is clearly in love with you, is just . . . clueless on your part. And that you could blow off Emily's party when she adores you, is selfish and thoughtless. I need a man who puts his family first. Not a guy who refuses to engage his heart in order to protect it from ever getting hurt!"

Direct hit. But she was the first to make him want to chance being hurt.

He held his hands out and pleaded, "I'm sorry, Shelby. I never meant to hurt you. I'll do anything to make things right. To prove that I love you."

"Love me?" The dam broke and Shelby's tears streamed down her face again. She made a choking sound before she turned and opened her car door. After she slipped inside she said quietly, "Words, Nick. You're good at using them, but you don't have any idea what they really mean. We're done."

As Shelby drove away, his throat constricted. He'd just lost the only woman he'd ever loved.

He'd forgotten Lori and Jo were still there until his sister said, "Why did you spy on her business, Nick?"

He met Lori's icy stare. "Grandma asked me to help you save your matchmaking business."

"I was afraid of that." Lori crossed her arms and huffed out a breath. "If you'd had the consideration to talk to me, rather than doing this behind everyone's back, you would have figured out I sold my client list to Dating.com the day I asked you to take Em to the bookstore. There's no business to save, Nick."

"What?" The air whooshed from his lungs. "How could you have done that? You love being a matchmaker."

"I need to support Emily on my own now. I made enough money from the sale so I can finish up my degree. I don't have the luxury of doing what I love for a living . . . like you evidently do. But then, I'd never let my job become more important than my family, so maybe it's best this way. Have fun with your client this weekend. Emily will get over it . . . eventually."

Jo sent him a frown as she turned and followed his sister back into the café, leaving him standing in the middle of the parking lot. Alone.

Digging out his keys, he slowly trudged to his car and got in. He'd let them all down. Shelby, his grandmother, Lori, and even Emily.

A complete fail.

He laid his forehead on the steering wheel and closed his eyes.

Maybe he *was* better off being single and avoiding relationships like before. Shelby was right. He'd just hurt everyone in his life he cared for—just like his father had.

16

"Losing Julie gave Chester a sore heart."
Chester is a Sad, Sad Monkey

Shelby, curled up on top of her bedspread with her knees drawn to her chest, moaned. She'd cried so hard the past few hours, there was nothing left.

Having your soul ripped out hurt.

She'd allow herself to wallow for a day or two, but no longer than that. She was a tough woman, one no man could destroy. But how could she have been so blind?

On a sob she gave in to the truth. She wasn't tough at all. More like humiliated, defeated, and right back to that same insecure-about-her-legs-and-unworthy-of-love girl she'd been before she'd met Nick. Worse, now she knew what it felt like to feel beautiful and loved by a man. Even if it had only been for a day and hadn't been real. She'd be so much better off if she'd never known.

Maybe if she pretended to be strong it'd eventually become true?

She should have listened when Nick had told her straight up he didn't date because he didn't want marriage and a family. He wasn't ever planning to have a real relationship with her, he just wanted to sleep with her.

She deserved a man who wanted the same things she did. Maybe seeing Nick's true colors saved her from worse heartache later.

Thank God she hadn't told him she loved him. That would've just made her look even more like the fool she was.

A quiet knock sounded on her bedroom door before Jo poked her head inside. "Hi."

Shelby rolled over and flopped onto her back. Staring up at the ceilings, she croaked out, "Hey."

The side of the bed sank with Jo's weight. "Have you eaten anything since breakfast? It's almost eight."

Shelby shook her head. "Not hungry."

"I figured you'd say that." Jo grabbed Shelby's hand and yanked. "Can't have you wasting away to nothing. Luckily, I know the one thing you can't resist."

Shelby let herself be dragged to the kitchen like a rag doll. When she got there, her eyes widened. "You made me a sundae bar?" There must've been twenty topping choices, including her all-time favorites: crushed Heath bars, M&M's, gummy bears, nuts, real whipped cream in the spray can, hot fudge, and chocolate sauce. There could never be enough variations of chocolate. But no cherries. She hated cherries. And best of all, chocolate shell for the top.

Jo smiled. "Best dinner ever, right?"

Shelby wrapped her arm around Jo's waist and squeezed. "You're the best *friend* ever." Thank goodness she had Jo. The only person who'd never let her down.

So, she'd ignore her queasy stomach and dig in, for Jo's sake.

Pooling chocolate sauce on the bottom of her oversized bowl, she alternated various chocolate layers with nuts, whipped cream, and ice cream. After she'd poured the chocolate shell over the top and let it set up, she sat at the table in the kitchen's nook, waiting for Jo to sit across from her. After tapping spoons, they dug in.

A few bites in, Shelby had to stop. She just couldn't do it.

Jo's forehead crumpled. "Really? Ice cream has always been your cure-all."

"I can't believe I was so wrong about him." Tears burned Shelby's eyes again. "I thought he was the one, Jo. He made me laugh like no one else. And he was the first guy who made me feel like my legs weren't so bad. But none of it was true. He'd just told me all of that to keep me around long enough to help his sister's business. He's not the happily-ever-after guy I'd fooled myself into thinking he was."

Jo frowned as she took another bite. "I know we'd still like to castrate Nick with a butter knife, but maybe I should tell you what happened after you left."

"What? Did Nick and Lori have a good old laugh at how gullible I am?"

"No, not at all. They were both pretty upset. From their conversation, I figured out Nick never told Lori anything about your business, because if he had, he would have known she'd sold hers."

"Lori sold her client list? I get asked that all the time. Please don't tell me she sold out to one of those stupid online giants. They're worthless."

"I can't remember the name, but yeah. It sounded like it. And something about their grandmother. And about disappointing Emily. It didn't end well between them. You'll be happy to know it looked like Nick had just taken a beating with a paddle in the principal's office by the time we left."

Shelby sighed. That *should* make her feel better. Instead she still just felt unbearably sad.

❦

Nick, tired of staring at his living room walls, needed dinner and a stiff drink. All he had was a jar of peanut butter in the cupboard and some light beer in the fridge. Not going to cut it.

Maybe he'd walk to the little Irish pub he'd been to a few times that sat on the corner just outside the subdivision's gate. It was better than wallowing alone in his guilt.

He grabbed his jacket and headed out. The pub owners, an older couple who'd emigrated from Ireland, bragged that the magic in their whiskey was potent and smooth enough to drown any kind of pain.

Just what he needed to forget about Shelby. Her finding out and ending things was for the best. As much as he'd tried to convince himself he could be what Shelby wanted, he'd just fooled himself. Shelby deserved the prince she'd waited for.

And a prince, he was not. He'd proved that earlier by alienating all the women in his life.

After his short walk, Nick yanked the wooden door open and stepped inside the cozy pub. Thursday nights must be slow ones. There were only two guys throwing darts in the back and a few couples sitting at tables. The last thing he wanted to do was sit at a table alone, so he headed for the bar.

Brian, the owner, lifted a hand. "Be right with ya."

Nick nodded and pulled out a stool. After Brian finished layering a proper Guinness and handed it out, he waddled over. "So, what's your pleasure this fine evenin'? Nick, isn't it? I never forget me a face."

"Nice to see you, Brian. A double dose of your magic whiskey, and a corned-beef sandwich, please."

Brian cocked his head as he poured out the drink. "I recall your fondness for the sandwich, but you're usually a beer man if my mind 'aint playin' tricks on me?"

Nick nodded. "Been a helluva day."

"So, would your troubles be business related or woman based? 'Tis usually one or the other."

Nick grunted. "Not just one, but four women. And one's not even alive."

"Well now, this can't be good." Brian chuckled. "I'll be sending ya down a free refill to help soothe the pain while me lovely wife fixes your sandwich."

"Thanks." Nick drank deeply before swinging his stool around to watch the dart game. As soon as he'd drained his glass Brian appeared with another drink.

After lifting it up as a toast in thanks, Nick took another long pull.

By the time his meal arrived he felt nice and numb all over. He made quick work of the sandwich and all the thick fries on the side.

Just as he wiped his mouth on his napkin and pushed his plate forward, Brian appeared with another drink. "Are ya drivin', son? If so, I'd have your keys and I'll call you a cab."

"Nope." Nick shook his head. "I'm on foot tonight."

Brian slid the drink closer. "Then, bottom's up it is."

Brian waited as Nick drained his glass. "I fancy myself a good judge of character. You strike me as a fine man, Nick. Want to talk about it?"

"There's where you'd be wrong." A bitter laughed escaped. "A fine man I'm not. I just screwed up the best thing I'd ever had. No one is talking to me because I've been an ass. Just like my father. That apple not falling far from the tree thing is real."

Brian stood patiently and listened as Nick spilled his guts to this virtual stranger. Something he'd never done before.

After he finished, Brian said, "I've been married going on forty years now. Can't say I understand women any better now than on me weddin' day. But seems to me, your heart was in the right place, ya just went and mucked it up real good. So, what are ya gonna do to fix it?"

Nick shook his head and started on the fresh drink Brian slid in front of him. "I don't have a flippin' clue."

"Oh, but ya do." Brian laughed. "Clearly 'tis love you have for each of them. Show 'em how much you're willin' to make an arse outta yourself. They love that the best. Women are odd that way. Write some silly poetry, or do something equally emasculating. The more humiliating, the quicker you'll win their hearts back, and they'll reward you with their pretty smiles. Especially your Shelby, there. She sounds like a woman worth a good fistfight. Am I right?"

Nick nodded. Shelby was worth it. Not that he'd win a fight in his current drunken state, but he couldn't let Greg have Shelby. Brian was right. Time to fight for what he wanted. He'd figure out the how-to-be-a-prince thing as he went along.

What *would* it take to make them smile?

He tossed all the cash in his wallet onto the bar and then stood to go home. "Thanks, Brian. I owe you one."

Brian smiled as he counted out the money. "It looks like we're more than even here." He slid a few bills back. "You're a truly fine man, Nick. Don't listen to the daemons inside who tell ya otherwise. Hope to see ya soon. Love to hear how it all went."

"You got it. 'Nite." Nick smiled as he weaved his way to the door. Maybe there was magic in that Irish whiskey yet.

∽

Shelby sat next to Jo on the couch in their living room. With both their hands reaching in unison into the almost-empty bowl of buttered popcorn between them, they sighed as the ending credits scrolled for *While You Were Sleeping*.

She'd been weepy all day. Watching romantic movies probably wasn't such a great idea. But she liked seeing other people get the happily ever after she hoped for herself one day.

Jo asked, "One more movie?"

"Why not? Let's make our wild Friday night even better by shedding more tears."

Jo smiled and topped off Shelby's wine glass. "So, Emily's birthday party is tomorrow, right? You up for spending the day with Nick's family?"

"No. But I can't hurt Emily. I have to go. Besides, I'm almost over him."

Jo pointed to the stack of crumpled tissues on the coffee table. "That movie was a romantic comedy, not a tear-jerker, Shelby. You're not even close to over him."

"Okay. You're right. But it's so annoying." Shelby pulled her legs up to her chest and wrapped her arms around them. Laying her chin on her knees, she said, "Today I've shifted to being madder at myself than I am at Nick. I *knew* better, Jo. I've always steered clear of guys like Nick. I let his good looks cloud my judgment, like a silly teenager. I deserve all this pain. I'll be sure to relive it if ever I'm tempted like that again."

"Maybe you're being a little too hard on yourself, Shelby. You've been really happy these last few weeks with Nick. It wasn't just his looks. It ran deeper than that."

"Maybe. But Nick is still the wrong guy for me in the long run. Emily is a good example. Nick missing her birthday party, putting work before her, will break her heart. She really loves him. And he knows it, yet he still made the choice he did. This way is better."

Jo found *Pride and Prejudice* in the on-demand list and hit the play button. "I'm not on Nick's side or anything, but he cared enough for you to find that fire report and help rid you of all that guilt about your family. That's a Mr. Darcy move, for sure. I think there's more to this story than you know. And may I point out, Elizabeth Bennet doesn't like Darcy at first either. Then there was a bit of a misunderstanding about his behavior, but let's watch and see what happens."

"Funny." She closed her eyes and sighed. She knew how the story went. After they'd sorted out their mix-up, Elizabeth realizes she was too quick to judge Darcy without all the facts. Then the happily ever after ensues. But hearing whatever lame excuse Nick came up with wouldn't change the fact that they just didn't want the same things and were never meant to be.

Stupid tears burned her eyes again.

Her happily ever after wasn't coming anytime soon, so she settled in, determined to take her mind off Nick and enjoy the movie. It was one of her favorites.

After a half hour, she couldn't stand it any longer. Darn Jo for making the reference between Nick and Mr. Darcy. Every time Darcy came on screen, her mind filled with images of

Nick, all annoyingly handsome and perfect. "I'm gonna hit the hay. See you in the morning."

Jo smiled. "Sweet dreams . . . Miss Bennet."

"Ha-ha. If you weren't my best friend, I'd . . ." She was pathetic. She was such a sad-sack she couldn't even muster a decent comeback.

Crawling under her covers, she squeezed her eyes shut and counted from one thousand backward, praying it'd block all the thoughts of Nick and Mr. Darcy bouncing around in her head.

༄

Shelby hitched up the strap of the bag of books on her shoulder and shifted Emily's gift to her other hand. She could handle a simple birthday party for a kid. She opened the glass door and entered . . . mayhem. The loud, happy screeches of kids playing video games blended with the electronic bleeps and blips. Six-foot-tall furry woodland characters mingled and took pictures with the children.

The scent of sugar and greasy pizza body-slammed her. The noise and the smell weren't going to help the stress headache that gripped the base of her skull like a vise.

She forced her feet to venture farther inside, wading through smiling kids running around with fists filled with tickets. There must've been four or five parties going on at the same time. There were people everywhere. The place was packed.

After finally spotting Lori and her parents at the rear, Shelby headed their way.

She added to the pile of gifts on the table marked with Emily's name then sucked in a deep breath for courage before turning to greet everyone. Before she could say hello, Nick's mom stood and held her arms wide for a hug. "Hi, Shelby, thank you so much for coming." Linda wrapped her arms around Shelby and whispered, "I know it's not easy for you to be here. Nick told us what a dope he'd been. But we're all so happy you decided to come."

Relieved, because she'd fear they'd all take his side, she finally smiled. "Emily's my favorite fan. I wouldn't have missed it for the world."

Lori said, "Come sit and visit with us for a minute while the kids are playing games. It may be the only chance we have at some semblance of peace for the rest of the afternoon."

Shelby waved to Nick's dad, who was busy assembling a toy, then slid on the bench next to Lori. "I'm sorry about the other day—"

"Nope." Lori held up her hand. "I understand. Beth purposely made it sound like she and Nick were going on a date, of course you were upset. I was mad at Nick too, until I calmed down a bit and thought about it. Nick was just being . . . Nick. He can be kinda clueless sometimes, but he actually meant well with the spying."

Meant well? *Was* she pulling an Elizabeth Bennet on Nick? Jo said there might be more to the story.

Didn't matter. Nick wasn't the right guy, as much as her heart kept telling her so, she needed to listen to her sensible brain.

Emily ran toward her with her arms spread wide. "Hi, Shelby."

She lifted Emily up and gave her a tight hug. "Hi, Em. Happy birthday! Are you having fun?"

Emily nodded "Yeah. But I miss Uncle Nick."

"I know, kiddo. But hey"—Shelby lifted her bag of books—"wanna pick out which books to give to your friends and then I'll sign them?"

"Okay." A big smile formed on Em's face as she dug through the bag. Lori wrangled all the little girls and managed to organize a line.

Em, seated on Shelby's lap and excited to help, held the book open to the right page for her to sign. Emily's hair smelled like Johnson's baby shampoo and something sweet, a little like . . . cake. Shelby drew a deep breath and imprinted the memory. She hated that she probably wouldn't see Em much anymore.

Just as she signed the last book, Emily pointed and screeched, "Look. It's Chester!"

When Shelby spotted the six-foot-tall monkey carrying a present, she smiled. She hadn't seen that character when she'd come in. Must be part of the birthday package Nick paid for. It was nice he thought to get Emily a monkey that looked so much like Chester.

Emily squiggled out of Shelby's lap and dropped to the floor. She ran full tilt toward the monkey, dodging all the other kids in her path. The monkey leaned down and opened its arms wide. Emily screeched with joy as the monkey picked her up and swung her around.

As depressed as Shelby had been the last few days, it felt good to smile. The happiness on Emily's face made it hard not to. Maybe this place wasn't so bad after all.

After the monkey set Em down, he handed her the present at his feet. She picked it up and added it to all the others on her table. "Mommy, Chester is going to play games with us now."

"Okay, have fun." Lori waved at Emily as she slid next to Shelby on the aluminum bench. All the kids gathered around the monkey, who picked each of them up and gave them a big twirl. "Nick must've really been feeling guilty about missing the party. That monkey had to cost a bunch extra."

Shelby shrugged. "Yeah, but he needs to learn he can't throw money at a situation and make it better. He should've made the effort to be here."

Lori's mom and dad joined them. Linda said, "I totally agree. This is a fun party, Lori."

When the monkey picked Emily up and carried her over to the skeeball machines, Shelby turned to Lori. "So, Jo mentioned something about you selling your client list?"

Lori nodded. "I loved being a matchmaker, but life got in the way. I needed to make more than my business was pulling in to be sure Em can go to college one day. But I'll really miss the people. And proving my gut feelings were right when they end up together. You know the feeling, right?"

Shelby shook her head. "I don't have the gut thing, my matches are based on algorithms. But I know what you mean about the excitement of matching the right people. It's an awesome feeling to be a part of that."

"I had a good feeling about you and Nick." She held a hand out in her parents' direction. "We're all sorry things didn't work out."

"Yeah." Shelby sighed. "Me too."

Nick had the nicest family. It always made her heart ache a little when she spent time with them. Since losing hers, she'd always longed to be a part of a family again. But that wasn't happening anytime soon.

Suddenly the monkey and Emily appeared in front of Lori. A muffled voice from inside said, "This is for you, Emily's mom."

"A present for me?" She reached out and peeked inside the big gift bag the monkey held out. Lori pulled out a stack of papers, frowning as she studied the note attached.

"What have you got there, Lori?" Nick's dad asked.

"It's my client list." Lori's head whipped up and she blinked at the monkey. "How could . . ."

The monkey lifted his hands and removed the headpiece.

Emily screamed, "Uncle Nick is Chester! I thought you had to work?"

Nick's family all smiled as Nick picked Em up and gave her a hug. "I couldn't miss your party, Em. I let someone else handle my work."

Then he turned to Lori. "You need to do what you love, Lori. It makes you happy. I'm sorry I tried to fix things behind your back. Won't happen again. We'll find a way for you to go to school and keep this too. Okay?"

Lori blinked back her tears as she pulled the bundle of papers to her chest. "Thank you, Nick."

The raw emotion on Lori's face thawed Shelby's frozen heart a few degrees.

Nick had actually come through and chosen his sister and Emily over work. Good for him. Maybe he *had* changed a little.

When Nick's eyes met hers, his smile slowly faded. The unhappiness written all over his face tugged at her soul.

Lori quickly pulled herself together and reached out for Emily. "Let's go get some more cake everyone, so Nick can speak to Shelby."

Emily frowned. "But he wants cake too." She turned to him. "Right, Uncle Nick?"

He handed Em over and forced a smile. "I'll be there in a minute. Save me some okay?"

Lori and her family quickly disappeared and then it was just the two of them, staring at each other, surrounded by screaming kids.

Butterflies took flight in her gut as she rose from the aluminum bench. "Hi."

"Can we talk, please?"

She could only nod because her throat was so clogged with emotion.

Part of her wanted to run, afraid he'd hurt her again, but the dark shadows under his eyes stopped her eager feet. He probably hadn't slept a full night either and looked as miserable as she felt.

He glanced around. "Too loud in here. Let's go outside."

She cleared her throat. "Give me a second."

He shifted his weight impatiently from foot to foot while she called out and waved goodbye to everyone. She'd have liked to give them all one last hug, but she'd lose it if she did.

She'd just gathered her things when he wrapped his rubber monkey hand around her arm and motored her toward the front door. That was a bad habit of his, dragging her around like that. But like the "dammit, Shelby," it had sort of grown on her.

Once outside, the silence was golden. She glanced up at him. As angry and hurt as she was, Nick dragging her around while dressed in three-quarters of a monkey suit threatened to make her smile. That was something she'd never imagined seeing.

He said, "I'm really sorry, Shelby. I should've come clean a lot sooner. And I meant what I'd said about us not being a one-night stand. I've cared for you from the start."

"You don't spy on people you care about. And you especially don't sleep with them while spying. You hurt me, Nick."

"I didn't mean to. At first I didn't know how to tell you, then I considered not telling you because I'd decided not to give the data to my sister. But then I realized you needed to know, so I'd planned to take you to dinner and explain things." Still hauling her toward the huge parking lot he asked, "Where are you parked?"

"Over there." She beeped her key fob. Her flashing headlights gave him his answer. She might as well get the whole story out of him. "So, why were you spying on me and what did you hope to learn?"

He stopped walking and shifted the monkey head to his other arm. "Lori's matchmaking business has been handed down from generation to generation in my family. The day my grandmother died, she begged me to make sure the business was still there for when Emily grew up—if she wanted it." His hairy monkey-suit arm slipped around her shoulder as he guided her toward her car again. "You use computers, databases, social media and Lori uses index cards just like my grandmother did. Lori needed to keep up, or the business would disappear. I wanted to see how you did it so I could teach her."

She'd spent many hours designing her systems, and they worked well. "But Lori's way has merit too, even if it doesn't earn as much money. Hiring a part-time kid with computer skills would have been a simpler way to fix it rather than spying on me."

He stopped dead in his tracks and frowned. The befuddlement on his face was sorta cute. He finally said, "That's exactly what she needs to solve her problems and keep the business alive, maybe if you and Lori combined your . . ." He frowned and cut himself off. "Sorry." He moved his hand to her lower back and gently guided her to her car again. "Lori's deal, not mine. I need to stay out of it."

His remorse *seemed* genuine.

He'd spied to keep a promise to his grandmother. But he hadn't gone through with it. He hadn't been involved with Beth. He came through for Emily and Lori in the end, but was he honestly ready for a real relationship? The compromises, the sacrifices. A family?

Did she really want to take that big a risk with her heart?

But then, Nick had donned a monkey suit. That had to count for *something*.

When they got to her car, and she'd tossed her things onto the passenger seat, she turned to him. "Let's say I decide to forgive you, which I haven't yet. What do you want from me, Nick?"

He plopped the monkey head on top of her car. "A fresh start, Shelby. Please? Clean slate and a date. I'll be waiting for you at that Italian place we went to before. See you at seven."

Before she could reply, he turned to go, the arrogant monkey. Always so sure of himself. And he'd forgotten his head.

He must've realized it, because he turned around and marched toward her again. He stopped in front of her and slipped his rubber hands along the sides of her face and lifted it up. Then he laid his soft lips on hers and kissed her so sweetly her heart sighed.

When his lips slowly left hers, she blinked open her eyes and stared into his darkened ones as he whispered, "I want *you*, Shelby. Forever." Then he grabbed his head and strode back toward the party.

Who does that? Drops a "Forever" bomb and just walks away?

Nick Caldwell, that's who.

She opened her car door and slipped behind the wheel.

Maybe she didn't feel like Italian. Had he thought about that? No! He just did his stupid Neanderthal thing and expected her to fall right in line, as usual. How apropos he'd been wearing a monkey suit while doing it. The big ape.

But the thought of that lasagna made her mouth water. If she went, he'd have to spring for a good bottle of wine. And dessert too, dammit.

Still shaking her head, she started her car and put it in gear.

Nick was the most impossible man she'd ever met. So what would she do with him? Forever.

17

"Chester loves Julie ten times more than bananas. But did she love him back?"
Chester Gets His Favorite Thing

Nick waited at a table in the rear of the warm restaurant, his back to the wall, watching and praying Shelby wouldn't stand him up. It was seven o'clock. One of Shelby's rules of dating was never be late. But he didn't care, as long as she showed.

At five minutes after seven the doors swung open and a group of six big men crowded in along with a gust of cool air from outside. They mingled up front while waiting to be seated. He craned his neck, searching and hoping she slipped in behind them. But no sign of her.

Shelby being late wasn't good. He should've told her he loved her again. Why had he forgotten that part? And all the other stuff he'd planned to say?

He could text her to be sure she was coming, but then she'd be mad at him for using his phone instead of pretending to wait for that magical-moment thing she said was supposed to happen when they first see each other. He couldn't afford to make her any angrier.

Five minutes later, another rush of cold air swirled in, but the people gathered up front still stood in the way. He couldn't see who had entered.

Shelby suddenly appeared, slipping between two of the waiting men, and then swiveled her head, searching for him.

She'd come.

He swiped his napkin from his lap and stood so she could see him. When their eyes met she smiled. He felt the impact like a hot laser pulse to his gut. So it was real after all? Did she feel it too?

Shelby weaved through the tables, making her way toward him as she unbuttoned her coat. She had on the same outfit she'd worn the first time they'd met. That had to be a good sign, right? Like a do-over?

He'd be sure to mention it. Showing he paid attention. Or was it a bad thing to point out an outfit a woman wore twice? Dammit. Maybe he should just keep his yap shut about it and pretend they'd never met? He'd asked her for a clean slate, after all.

He pulled out her chair. "Hi, I'm Nick. Shelby described you perfectly. I'd know you anywhere, Summer."

She lay her tiny purse on the empty seat beside her. "Nice opening. You get a point for that."

Relief washed through him. Maybe she *was* going to give him another chance.

He took her coat and lay it by her purse, then helped her get settled. Wiping his sweaty palms on his slacks, he took his place across from her. "Thanks for coming. I was afraid you'd changed your mind."

"Changed my mind? That would imply you actually gave me a choice. Which you didn't. You just *told* me to be here. So, I was sitting in the car debating. Then I got hungry. I hear the lasagna is good here."

"Sorry. I was afraid you'd say no if I gave you a choice." Panic took root in his gut again. Maybe she wasn't taking him back? He'd better step up his game. Shelby's dating handbook said to ask probing questions and show interest in the answer. "So, what do you do for a living, Summer?"

As Shelby stared into his eyes, as if deciding if she wanted to play along with the clean-slate game, his heart nearly stopped beating.

Then that mischievous grin he loved so much formed. "Well, I recently made a big life change. Like our pal Lisa, I felt stifled in my job as a writer, so I decided to compete with her and started an online shop. We sell spooky crystals and have a large selection of voodoo dolls. Along with all the ingredients you'd need for any spell you'd like to conjure."

"Is that so?" He laughed and leaned closer. "Know any good *love* spells?"

"I might be willing to brew one up . . . for you." Shelby closed the distance between them and gave him a soft kiss. "But if you screw up again, watch out. I have a voodoo doll with your name on it, pal. I'd keep the monkey suit too, if I were you."

~

A few months later . . .

Shelby leaned closer to the bathroom mirror as she swiped on mascara. Nick's voice from downstairs bellowed, "Dammit, Shelby. We're late!"

She yelled back, "Haven't you learned by now that screaming at me doesn't make me go any faster?" She got back to business and applied liner. She was behind because she'd torn the bathroom apart looking for her birth control pills. She couldn't imagine how she'd misplaced them. They always sat in the same place on her side of Nick's enormous granite counter top in their bathroom.

The next thing she knew, she was upside down and over Nick's big shoulder. "Time's up. You can finish in the car."

"Nice. Now my hair is messed up." After he pressed her makeup bag into her hand, she sent the pointy tip of her shoe into his gut and got a respectable grunt out of him. "Have you seen my pills? I can't find them."

"Worry about the pills later, we don't want to be late for the party."

"Then stop by the *wrong* side of the bed and lean down so I can grab my cell off my nightstand, Mr. Impatient." Since they both were used to sleeping on the right side of the bed, she'd agreed to flip a coin for it. And she'd lost.

After he complied, they headed down the stairs and she poked him in the ribs. "You're going to care about those pills later tonight, buddy. No pills, no nooky."

He pushed open the door from the house to the garage. "You're just still mad I got my way with the best side of the bed." He plopped her down beside the Porsche, kissed her deeply, then opened her door.

Still a little dizzy from his fantastic kiss, she said, "Yeah, that too."

She shook her head and slipped inside. As he backed out of the garage, she flipped down the mirror. After applying gloss, she smacked her lips, finger combed her hair, and then slapped the mirror closed.

Truth was, she was getting used to the wrong side of the bed, so it hadn't been such a bad compromise. Not that she'd share that little detail with him.

She needed to put her latest plan into action. They'd been dating for eight months, she'd been living with him for the last five, and that was long enough.

She'd tried leaving pictures of her favorite rings from Tiffany's on the coffee table and in his study, and dropping hints about how it'd be perfect to have a destination wedding in Italy in August or September when the weather would be the best. It being July, Mr. Thick Headed apparently hadn't caught on.

"So, Jo said something interesting today. She suggested since I wasn't living in my house anymore but still paying the mortgage, wouldn't it be smarter for me to sell her the house? Then she'll find a roommate to offset her expenses. But that'd mean I'd have nowhere to live if you kicked me to the curb."

Nick laughed. "That's rich. If anyone does the kicking in this relationship it's you." He rubbed his belly, reminding her of her earlier actions.

"That was more a poke than a kick." She stifled her grin. "So what do you think I should do?"

"Whatever you want, Shelby. It's your house, but it does seem like a waste to pay all that money when you can live with me for free."

She should've kicked him a lot harder. "Look at this from my perspective. I'm just a guest in your home. What if you get tired of me and I've already sold my house to Jo who has a new roommate? Where would I go?"

He shrugged. "Jo has a couch. Or your aunt and uncle's?"

She wanted to belt him. "Okay, Blockhead. This would be a good time to say something like, 'Shelby, I love you. I want to spend the rest of my life with you, blah, blah.'"

He chuckled as they pulled into his mother's driveway. "Calm down, Shelby. We'll talk about this later."

She got out of the car and slammed her door. Then she marched inside. After she doled out hugs to everyone, she turned to Nick's Mom. "Hi. Happy Fourth of July." Shelby hugged Nick's mom really hard and then kissed her cheek. She really loved Linda. "How can you be so great but have such a slow-witted son?"

Linda leaned back and frowned. "What's wrong, honey?"

"Nothing my bat won't cure when we get home." Shelby took a deep breath and tried to shake it off.

Linda smiled as she pushed a glass of wine into Shelby's hand. "You'll be singing a different tune by the end of the night, sweetheart. I promise."

"Doubt it." She frowned as she took a long pull from her glass.

After a great BBQ dinner, they all sat around the backyard eating dessert, waiting for the fireworks to begin.

Shelby's mood had lightened a little. Mostly because she'd decided Nick wasn't getting any tonight even if he begged. Maybe even for the whole weekend. If she could hold out that long.

Oh, who was she kidding? She was pudding in his hands, but she could make him pay for one night at least.

Everyone had plates of watermelon in their laps when Emily ran toward her. "Shelby, me and Uncle Nick wrote a book for you."

She laid her plate aside and pulled Emily onto her lap. "You did?"

Emily beamed a bright smile. "Yeah, I did the pictures, Uncle Nick wrote the words on the computer and momma took it someplace and they put the pink metal things in to hold it together."

She glanced at Nick, who had a smug grin on his face. "You aren't the only one who can write great books, Shelby."

She accepted the adorable book and sighed. *"Ten things Nick and Emily Love about Summer Sinclair."*

They'd used her real name. She blinked back her threatening tears.

Emily hopped up and down on her lap. "We both got five things. Mine are first."

"Ladies first, that makes sense." Shelby laid a kiss on the top of Emily's head. "Thank you, sweetheart."

She opened the book and grinned at the crude illustrations. "This is pretty great. I'm worried you guys are going to outsell me."

Nick slipped beside her on the picnic bench and pulled her close. "This is the time *I'm* choosing to tell you that I love you Shelby and that I want to spend the rest of my life with you, blah, blah." He kissed her cheek. "Here's the blah, blah part."

Tears blurred her vision as she hurried through Emily's sweet pages. They were awesome, but she was dying to see what Nick had come up with.

When she'd turned Emily's fifth page she said, "Thank you, Monkey-Brains, I love you too." She kissed Emily and then handed her over to Lori who'd moved beside her, smart enough to realize what was coming next was something a person didn't want to do with a kid on her lap.

She turned the next page, grinning in anticipation. Reading aloud for the group, she said, "Number six. Nick loves how Summer makes him feel when she's with him. It's even better than when he's enjoying a cold beer and a plate of loaded nachos at a Broncos game."

Shelby glanced at Nick and cocked a brow.

He laughed. "They get better, keep going."

Chuckling, because nachos and beer at a Broncos game were a pretty great thing, she turned the page.

"Number seven. Nick loves how Summer smiles at kids. He wants three as soon as possible because she'll be as great a mom as his own."

Nick's mom beamed a huge smile. "Thank you, Nick." Then she turned to Shelby. "He's right, Shelby. And I can't wait to be a grandmother again."

Nick's dad agreed.

Shelby turned and met Nick's gaze, probably grinning like an idiot. They'd never talked numbers, just that they wanted kids. She'd been too busy concentrating on the getting-him-to-marry-her part.

"Really? You want three?"

He nodded. "Is that too many? We can negotiate."

She kissed him. "No, three is perfect. And you're right. These are getting better."

Flipping over the next page, she read, "Number eight. Nick loves Summer's legs. He's always reminded of what a brave woman Summer is when he sees them. She's the most beautiful woman Nick has ever known. Inside and out."

She found Nick's hand and gave it a hard squeeze. She had to bite her bottom lip to stop the tears that threatened again. He couldn't have said anything to touch her more deeply.

It didn't matter what came next. All she knew was that she wanted to spend the rest of her life with such a wonderful, clueless caveman.

Still holding Nick's hand, she cleared her throat. "Number nine. Nick loves the way Summer compromises. Nick's really loving having his side of the bed back."

She laughed. That was what was so great about them. He knew she'd be all choked up after his comments about her legs so he'd made a joke. They truly got each other.

Playing along she whispered, "You just caught me at a weak moment. Don't expect any more compromising in the future, buddy."

He slipped his hand from hers and slid it around her shoulder. His warm breath whispered against her ear, "We'll see. Maybe you shouldn't read the last one out loud."

"Okay." She turned the page. Number Ten. *Nick plans to keep Summer naked for two solid weeks if she says "yes" to his next question.*

A slow smile stretched her lips as Nick slid off the bench and knelt before her. He dug through his pocket and pulled out a little blue Tiffany's box. Tilting the lid back he said, "I want you, Chester, and all the kids we'll be lucky enough to make to live together happily ever after, Shelby. I know I'm no prince, but will you marry me? Please?"

Everyone cheered as she grinned and snatched the box from his hand. Slipping the ring onto her finger she fought the urge to jump up and down like Emily and Chester often did.

"This is the ring I wanted the most!"

Nick rolled his eyes. "It was the biggest and most expensive of the five pictures you placed strategically around our house, so I figured."

Our house? Nice. "Thank you, babe." She pulled Nick's face to hers and laid her smiling lips on his. But as she kissed him, a thought occurred to her. She leaned back and whispered, "Did you steal my pills? You said you were in a hurry to have kids, but I'm not walking down the aisle with a baby bump."

"Yeah, but how long does the bump take to show? Because Jo, Lori, and I have been making plans for a destination wedding in Florence, per your numerous hints. If you approve, we all leave in a few weeks, the optimum time—per the printouts!"

Her heart swelled so big, she feared it'd pop. "So you were paying attention after all?"

"Really, Shelby? You can be about as subtle as a gun."

"But you love that about me, right?"

"Nope. Not a bit." Nick kissed her and then grinned as his lips slowly parted with hers. "But I love you for all the other stuff. So, is that a yes?"

"Yes!" Finally. Next stop—Italy—and then the chance to spend the rest of her life with the most handsome, annoying, wonderful man in the world. She couldn't wait to get started.

ACKNOWLEDGMENTS

This story was originally titled *Cyrano At Your Service* and won a prestigious award from The Romance Writer's of America®. It was responsible for the start of my professional writing career, yet it got pushed aside when market demands changed. Deadlines happened and contracts were signed while this story stood patiently by, waiting for me to come back to it and give it the love it deserved. It has seen many transformations, but the heart of the story never changed—love is full of surprises and comes when we least expect it.

Thank you to all who helped along the way. My patient critique group, Shea Berkley, Louise Bergin, and Robin Perini are simply the best. And thanks to my agent, Jill Marsal, for believing in this book and in me. It's always more fun when you have team support, and I'm blessed to have these ladies, along with my wonderful family, always at my side. And a special thanks to Monique for your ideas and support, along with all the creative things you continue to do for me.

And as always, thanks to my readers, for without you, none of the words matter.

ABOUT THE AUTHOR

Tamra Baumann is an award-winning author who writes light-hearted contemporary romance. Always a voracious reader, she picked up her first romance novel off the bestseller table in her favorite bookstore and was forever hooked. (Thank you, Nora Roberts!)

She lives in the Southwest, where the sun shines almost every day and the sunsets steal her breath away. She has two kids, both bilingual in English and sarcasm, and a dog who is addicted to Claritin because he's allergic to grass. Her husband, who gamely tolerates her many book boyfriends, has been her real-life boyfriend for more than thirty years.

Stop by and say hi at www.tamrabaumann.com.

Printed in Great Britain
by Amazon